Winning the
Billionaire

Also by JM Stewart

Bidding on the Billionaire

Winning the Billionaire

JM STEWART

New York Boston

Copyright © 2016 by JM Stewart
Excerpt from *Bargaining for the Billionaire* © 2016 by JM Stewart
Cover design by Elizabeth Turner
Cover image © Georgeijevic/istockphoto
Cover copyright © 2016 by Hachette Book Group, Inc.

Forever Yours
Hachette Book Group
1290 Avenue of the Americas
New York, NY 10104
forever-romance.com
twitter.com/foreverromance

First Edition: June 2016
Forever Yours is an imprint of Grand Central Publishing.
The Forever Yours name and logo are trademarks of Hachette Book Group, Inc.

The publisher is not responsible for websites (or their content) that are not owned by the publisher.

The Hachette Speakers Bureau provides a wide range of authors for speaking events. To find out more, go to www.hachettespeakersbureau.com or call (866) 376-6591.

ISBN 978-1-4555-9220-3 (ebook edition)
ISBN 978-1-4555-9221-0 (print on demand edition)

I dedicate this one to all the authors out there. For taking your dreams, your fantasies, your hearts and souls, and being brave enough to send them out into the world. Without a love for getting lost in your stories, I'm not sure I would've started writing. Thanks for your inspiration.

Winning the
Billionaire

Chapter One

Christina McKenzie tried to close her mouth, to force herself to blink. Common courtesy said she ought to at least turn around. She needed to do something other than stare. Staring was rude. So was drooling. She was pretty sure she was doing both. Her limbs, however, refused to obey. The sight before her had her Jimmy Choo's glued to the hardwood floor beneath her feet. The heat in the private vestibule she stood in ramped up a thousand degrees and perspiration prickled along her skin.

God almighty. Since she was fifteen she'd fantasized about this. On the other side of the threshold, Sebastian Blake stood with his arms folded, wearing a pair of stark-white snug-fitting boxers.

And nothing else.

It didn't help that his dark brown hair stuck up at odd angles. He looked like he'd just rolled out of bed, completing the fantasy running a loop in her head. The one starring him, having just rolled out of *her* bed.

She'd known Sebastian for over twenty years, since that fateful day on the playground in first grade when he'd bumped her out of the way to get to the monkey bars. He and her twin brother, Caden, had been joined at the hip since. Oh, she'd seen him with his shirt off plenty of times over the years. She'd never seen him quite like this, however, one tiny little scrap of fabric from being stark naked, and her imagination filled in the gaps fine, thank you very much.

She bit her bottom lip. God bless America. "Baz," as she'd been calling him since somewhere around second grade, had to be the finest specimen of the masculine form she'd ever seen. Six foot four inches of lean, sculpted muscle. A broad chest and wide shoulders tapered to lean hips and long legs. Every inch of him toned to perfection. She knew from experience he worked out religiously, because she went running with him on occasion. Sebastian lived by his routines. Standing there, soaking in every luscious inch of him, she was suddenly grateful for it. The man had well-defined pecs and a washboard stomach she ached to smooth her hands over.

"For the love of all that's holy, Tina, do you have to come over so damn early?" Sebastian leaned on the door frame.

The deep scowl etched into his forehead snapped the fantasy shut with the recoil of a rubber band, yanking her back to reality. One where hell would freeze over before he ever looked at her with anything more than feigned tolerance. Never mind she and Caden were fraternal twins or that, technically, she was older than both of them. Caden by thirteen minutes and Sebastian by four months. Sebastian tended to treat her like an annoying kid sister or at most a friend. Today, apparently, it was annoying sister.

One would think she'd be used to that look by now, but it grated her nerves every time. She was a woman. Damn it. Just once she wanted to see him acknowledge it.

Not that the desire was logical or that she had any intention of following it. Sebastian was a well-practiced playboy. He loved women. And often.

Soft fur brushed her ankle, announcing the presence of Spike, Sebastian's three-year-old tabby. Using Spike as an excuse to distract herself, she bent and scooped him off the floor. "Well, at least someone's happy to see me."

Purring loudly, Spike rubbed his face against her chin, and she stroked his head, pretending nonchalance as she turned her back to the door. If she didn't at least feign decorum, she'd lean over and lick Sebastian. God, how she longed to follow the trail of soft, dark hair straight into those boxers.

Desperate to save face, she shot a scowl over her shoulder. "It's eight a.m., Baz. You're usually up by now, and you could at least put pants on before answering the door. Where's Lupe?"

Lupe was Sebastian's housekeeper. She was a round little woman with a sharp mind and a soft heart. She was also the only person who could tolerate Sebastian's surly mood in the morning. Baz had had four housekeepers quit in the last two years alone. His crankiness, though, didn't seem to faze Lupe.

"I gave her the day off, and you're lucky I put anything on at all. It's been a long damn night. I've only been asleep for about an hour, and I hadn't intended to leave my bed until I have to get up for work tomorrow." He released a heavy breath. "Look, I'm exhausted. Is there something I can do for you?"

In two seconds flat, the meaning in his not-so-subtle words sank over her. Either Sebastian slept naked or he had a date, neither of which was a pleasing possibility. The former did nothing for the not-so-dry state of her panties. The latter made her chest ache for all the things she'd never have with him. Growing up, he'd spent so much time at her parents' estate in Redmond that her mother had practically adopted him. Every Christmas and Thanksgiving. Even the once-a-month family dinners on Sundays her mother insisted on. Sebastian was essentially family, like another brother.

She'd never gotten used to seeing him with other women, however, and her heart couldn't seem to accept he'd never see *her* as a woman.

She swallowed past a desert-dry throat and feigned indifference. "Hot date?"

Whatever good mood she'd started with this morning evaporated. The reaction rose every time she ran across Sebastian and one of his "groupies." Sebastian was a sworn bachelor, and his relationships were little more than a series of meaningless flings. His smile, though, could charm the pants off a hobo. Women flocked to him the way people did movie stars.

Christina bit her lower lip. Was one of those women still

asleep in his bed? Was that the reason he'd answered the door in his underwear? What she wouldn't have given once upon a time for him to look at *her* the way he looked at one of his groupies. A part of her still did.

"Work, Tina. It's the beginning of May. Summer is the busiest time of year for the resorts. The new couples' resort we opened in Italy isn't going according to plan, and it's been a really bad morning. Is there a reason you're on my doorstep this early or do you just enjoy coming over to annoy me?"

Tina. Nobody but Sebastian called her that. Caden called her Chris. Her parents called her by her given name. Sebastian had always called her Tina. When they were kids, he'd taunted her with the name, used it as a weapon. Now, every time he called her Tina, her heart clenched. Oh what she would give for him to whisper the nickname in her ear like a sweet nothing.

Annoyed by how easily he got to her, she shot a glare over her shoulder. "Pants, Sebastian."

He released an exasperated breath filled with barely contained restraint. "Fine. I'll protect your *delicate sensibilities* and go find some pants if you'll make me coffee. Aren't you usually at the office by now?"

The soft tap of his bare feet on the hardwood floors moved away from her, and Christina turned. He strode with casual ease farther into the condo, and her gaze set on the flex of his ass as he walked. God, he had the finest backside she'd ever seen, firm and round, and his boxers did nothing but showcase the length of his muscular legs.

Setting the thought aside with a sigh, she stepped across

the threshold and closed the door behind her, then put Spike on the floor. He brushed her ankle again before trailing after Sebastian, and Christina followed him inside.

"I have a meeting with my director of sales and marketing at ten, but I had some things I needed to do this morning." Namely, convince the city's favorite bachelor to participate in the auction again this year. "You know, you really need to learn how to make your own coffee, Baz."

The short entry hall she emerged from opened up into the main room, and she headed off to the kitchen on the left. Sebastian owned the penthouse in a premier condominium tower in downtown Seattle. The place was beautiful, modern extravagance without being overly flashy. Dark gray marble countertops and polished hardwood flooring. Floor-to-ceiling windows lined the far wall, allowing a spectacular view of the city, and a gorgeous stone fireplace separated the living room from the dining room. The décor had a distinctly homey feel to it, rich fabrics done in warm, earthy tones, but the place was too large for her taste.

They were different in that regard. Having grown up in a house big enough for twelve people, she preferred something a bit more quaint. She owned a modest-sized home away from the city. Her one luxury was her BMW. Okay, and her shoes. She had a love affair with designer heels. Half of her closet was filled with them.

Extravagant was all Sebastian, though. He was proud of his wealth and wasn't shy about showing it off, and he wanted the best of everything. Right down to his penthouse.

"Why? I've got people who do it for me." Sebastian

shrugged halfheartedly, moving with the long, smooth strides of a lanky cat as he strode toward the back of the condo.

To distract herself from the overwhelming desire to stand there and watch the flex of his ass again, Christina moved to the coffeepot on the far counter. As she set about brewing a pot of coffee, her thoughts went to her upcoming meeting with her director of sales and marketing at McKenzie Inc. She and Bob needed to discuss pricing for the next month's software release, especially since their closest competitor had been undercutting them lately.

By the time the hot liquid sputtered into the glass pot and the earthy aroma filled the air, Sebastian emerged from his bedroom. He now wore a pair of dark gray pajama bottoms that hung low on his hips. He hadn't put on a shirt, though, leaving her with a view of his spectacular chest.

She still had an insane desire to lick him. She'd long wondered if he had sensitive nipples and what sounds he'd make if she ran her tongue over one. So, she turned to the coffeepot, distracting herself with pouring him a steaming cup. She set the mug on the center island counter as he entered the kitchen.

Hair still sticking out at odd angles, he lifted the cup to his lips and took a sip before meeting her gaze with a weary sigh. "What do you need from me?"

Remembering the reason she'd come over in the first place, Christina put on her sweetest smile and clasped her hands together. "The bachelor auction's next month."

As head of a local charity foundation for breast cancer

research, she tried using the high-end auction to add a little fun to an otherwise heart-wrenching topic. Having lost
more than a couple members to the disease, her family in-
vested every year. Three years ago, she'd decided to try a
fund-raiser a bit off the beaten path, something that would
be sure to draw a crowd. What better way than gathering
Seattle's hottest bachelors? The first year the auction ran,
she'd invited friends, well-to-do women she knew liked to
let loose a little. The evening turned out to be a huge success and the event had taken on a life of its own. More
often than not, the women called wanting to know when
the next one was.

Baz was an auction favorite. As CEO and minority owner
of Blake Hotels and Resorts—a family-owned company
catering to relaxing but affordable vacations—he'd been la-
beled one of Seattle's most eligible bachelors three years in
a row. A local celebrity magazine did a spread ever year and
had nominated him. The article was what had spurred the
idea for the auction, and Baz had participated since its inception. He put on a flirty, playful act, and the women ate him
up. His bid alone last year brought in two million. Christina
had been getting calls for months wanting to know if he'd be
participating this year.

"Of course it is." Sebastian rolled his eyes, irritation crossing his features. He pushed away from the counter and
rounded the breakfast bar, taking his coffee with him as he
crossed to the windows lining the far wall.

She blinked, surprised by his reaction. He usually agreed
with a pleasant smile and *of course*. "I'm sorry to ask last

minute, but one of my guys had to drop out, and I'm short one bachelor. Are you busy?"

"I'm always busy." He waved a flippant hand over his shoulder, but his voice held little enthusiasm. "Whatever. I'll make time."

The odd, dispassionate tone of his voice nudged at her. Something was definitely off. This was cranky even for him. "If you're busy, I can find someone else…"

He spun to face her, eyes blazing. "I said I'd participate, all right? Are we done? I'm exhausted, my head is pounding, and I'd really like to go back to bed."

His harsh words hit that painful place inside, the one where she stuffed all those things she shouldn't be feeling for him anyway. The longing, the hurt…and the hopeless, unrequited love she couldn't let go of. Deep down, Sebastian was a good man. He worked hard. The resorts he and his father owned were the success they were because of him. He could always be counted on whenever she or Caden needed something.

Once again, though, he'd relegated her to the position of annoying kid sister. She wanted to scream at him. Or kiss him. Or take his hands and put them on her breasts. Maybe then he'd finally see her as a woman, flesh and blood and real. Goddammit.

She set her hands on her hips. "You know what? This is cranky even for you. Whatever the hell your problem is, take your bad mood out on someone else. I'm not your punching bag. Forget I asked. I'll find someone else. Grayson Lockwood owes me a favor anyway for saving his computer servers last year. Go back to whoever's waiting in your bed. If you had company, you could simply have said so."

Of course, she was rambling. He'd unseated her, the way he always did, and she'd snapped. Since grade school, Sebastian seemed to get a kick out of pushing her buttons, teasing her until she got mad. Having seen her through puberty and acne and her geeky college days, he knew every damn thing about her, which meant he knew every single hot button she had. And damn it, it always worked.

She snatched her purse off the counter, pivoted, and stalked from the kitchen. Outside of Caden and her father, Sebastian was the only man who held enough of her to break her heart. She'd fallen for him in high school, and hard as she tried to squash them, the emotions had only gotten stronger as the boy became a man. All because she'd seen his soft side when he thought nobody was looking. She'd watched him pluck his guitar and croon lonely ballads that brought tears to her eyes. Watched him lure Spike in off the street with a kind hand and patience. He had a heart in there somewhere, for all his infuriating cantankerous attitude, and it always managed to fill her with that schoolgirlish hope.

She firmly kept him in the realm of "delicious fantasy," though, and there he'd stay. She'd already fallen for one play-boy's charms. Four years ago when she discovered she wasn't the only love of Craig Lawson's life. That was a mistake she would not be repeating. Sebastian held too much of her al-ready.

Sebastian let out a heavy sigh behind her. "Tina, I'm too damned tired for this. Jesus. If you must know, I spent last night in the hospital in Everett and most of the morning with my father's lawyer. I only got home about an hour ago."

His words stopped her cold halfway to the entry hall. His father lived in Everett. Her irritation evaporated as alarm skittered up her spine. She spun to face him. He stood at the edge of the kitchen, free hand in his hair, holding the long bangs back off his forehead. His eyes, now that she'd stopped to really look at him, were red-rimmed and bloodshot. They filled with something resembling grief. She knew that look. It meant Sebastian's walls were crumbling. He'd had a very similar expression when his mother left all those years ago.

What on earth could shake him like this?

She stepped toward him, moving once again to the edge of the kitchen. "Something happened."

He dropped his arm to his side, his shoulders rounding with defeat. "My father had a massive heart attack Sunday night. We hoped he'd recover, but he didn't. He passed early this morning. So, whatever you need, add it to the list and go home. I'm not in the mood to fight with you. My only goal for today is to sleep."

Her heart clenched in sympathy. Sebastian and his father had never gotten along. Though he always brushed the tension off with rebellious dismissal, she'd seen the hurt in his eyes whenever the two men exchanged words. Sebastian coveted, but had never gotten, his father's approval. Suddenly his bad mood made all the sense in the world. He could be surly when he wasn't feeling well. If he fought grief on top of exhaustion?

She strode in his direction, depositing her purse on the

kitchen counter. "My God, Baz. Why didn't you call one of us? Even Mom or Dad would have come in a pinch. Are you all right? What can I do?"

Alarm scattered across his features right before his brow furrowed and his jaw tightened. He jabbed a finger in her direction and backed away from her like she held a hand grenade and had just pulled the pin. "Don't. Don't go all mother hen on me. I've got a lot of shit to deal with right now, and the last thing I need is you smothering me."

Sebastian hated when she "mothered" him, as he called it. She'd gotten the compulsive habit from her mother. Mom was a worrier, to the point she drove them all nuts sometimes. It had rubbed off over the years, if only because the constant attention to detail had always given Christina a sense of being cared for. She and Caden had always known that despite their parents' sometimes overwhelming demands for perfection, they were, above all, loved.

Christina moved in his direction anyway, stopping beside the breakfast bar. When push came to shove, Sebastian always stood up for her, had since high school. He'd teased her mercilessly sometimes but wouldn't allow anyone else to do the same. It had annoyed her, but it had also made her feel protected. She had to be there for him now. "You don't have to deal with this on your own, Baz. I know you. You're going to isolate, and it's not healthy."

"Damn it, Christina." He pivoted and stalked across the space between them, backed her against the counter behind her, and set his hands on either side of her. His eyes narrowed, his gaze hot and confrontational. "Go. Home."

More than a little surprised by his sudden nearness, she swallowed hard, her heart hammering a mile a minute. He was so close, his every breath whispered over her lips, warm, with a slight hint of mint that made her yearn to discover the flavor on his tongue. She ignored the intense desire to close the remaining inches between them and held her ground. This wasn't about her desire. He needed her, whether he wanted to admit it or not.

She angled her chin higher. "Or what? I'm not afraid of you. You can't boss me around."

What she expected from him, she couldn't be certain. They'd been butting heads since they were kids. She yelled, he yelled right back. She poked him in the chest; he poked her back. Sebastian liked to play the part of the bossy control freak, expecting her to bow to his demands. It made him good at his job.

If he wanted a fight, though, she'd give him one, because she knew him enough to know he would attempt to intimidate her. No doubt in order to get her to leave him alone to his misery. If a subject had anything to do with emotion, he avoided it as if it were a highly contagious disease. She'd never let the tactic work before, and she wouldn't now.

This time, though, he didn't do what she expected him to. Rather, his right hand slid into her hair, and before she could blink, he pulled her mouth to his. He didn't give her a chance to back away, to approve or deny his assault. His kiss wasn't fleeting, either, or soft and seductive, the way she'd always envisioned. His lips plied hers, tugging and demanding. His tongue stroked the seam of her mouth, a hot slide that had her gasping and opening for him. He took full advantage and swept in, his tongue restless in her mouth.

She whimpered. What she *needed* to do was push him away. He wasn't thinking clearly. He was lost in grief. Her body, however, didn't seem to be listening. His mouth was warm and luscious, and her arms wound themselves around his neck. How many times over the years had she imagined this moment? How many times had she stroked herself to orgasm fantasizing about his hands and his mouth on her body? Yet the reality far exceeded the fantasy, and God help her, she didn't have the strength to deny him.

Unfortunately, the fantasy didn't last long. As abruptly as he'd grabbed her, he released her. His breaths came harsh and shallow, his chest heaving in time with the fierce pounding of her heart.

"That's what. It's been a shitty day, Tina, and I'm feeling very ornery and very needy." As if to prove his point, he set his hands on the counter on either side of her and leaned into her, rocking his hips against hers.

The full press of his lean body against her had any thought of protest flitting away like wisps on a breeze. Sebastian was aroused, and his erection pressed into the softness of her stomach. He didn't feel like a small boy, either. She itched to reach down and stroke the length of his cock. She longed to put an end to the wondering and finally discover exactly how big he really was, yearned to know the soft, intimate heat of his skin.

The intensity of his stare held her trapped. Sapphires. He had eyes the colors of deep, brilliant sapphires. They were usually intense and focused. Right then, they were in full seduction mode. Never in a million years would she have thought to find herself on the receiving end of that captivating stare. She'd never been the kind of girl who went all tongue-tied over a man, who giggled and sighed. She was a woman in a male-dominated industry; she could hold her own with most men. But right then? God help her, she wanted to do exactly that: giggle like a giddy schoolgirl and beg him to fuck her senseless.

Damn it. He'd unseated her again. She desperately needed to regain her equilibrium. She was the CEO of a company *she'd* founded, with software *she'd* created. She'd always been the brain, top of her class. McKenzie Inc. was a success because of her dedication and determination, and she'd done it by herself, without any help from her parents. She was smart, not one of those party girls who dropped their panties simply because he looked like sex on legs.

She drew a shuddering breath, trying desperately to pull her wits about her. "I hate when you call me Tina."

It was such a stupid thing to say, but they were the only coherent words she could form. The nickname always rolled off his tongue like a sexy little pet name and drove her to distraction. She yearned for him to whisper the name in the dark…while he held her hands above her head and plunged deep inside her.

A soft bark of laughter rumbled out of him.

"And I hate when you call me Baz. I haven't been ten years old in a long time." His gaze flicked down her body and back up. "In case you haven't noticed, I've grown up. There's nothing small about me, sweetheart."

His words were a taunt, clearly meant to gain a reaction, but all Christina could do was close her eyes. Need shuddered through her, settling warm and wet between her thighs. Oh, she'd noticed all right. Every inch of her was currently aware of how little he *wasn't*. Sebastian had lit a fire in her belly no man could ever quench. Except him. This moment was a hot fantasy come to life. One she *needed* to resist or she'd be another one of his casualties. She'd end up like poor Jean.

The problem was, he was so close his warm breath caressed her cheek and her sense of logic went haywire.

Apparently not done tormenting her, he leaned his head beside her ear. His hot tongue traced a line up the side of her neck and ended with a flick to the underside of her earlobe. "You're not so immune. I can feel your every reaction. Every hitch in your breath and every shiver that runs through you. Admit it. You want me as much I want you."

Hot little shivers swept down her spine. She craved Sebastian like a starving man craved his next meal, and she was slowly losing this battle. "You're right, Baz. I won't deny it. I do want you. What woman in her right mind wouldn't?"

Oh, she tried hard not to judge him for the way he chose to deal with relationships. After all, she lived a similar life. Having discovered the guys in college all attempted to use her, she'd turned the game back on them. She couldn't blame Baz for living the same way. Doing so was easier than admitting no man had yet to see *her*. Her father owned one of the largest and oldest corporate law firms on the West Coast, and he came from old money. He was worth billions. All the men she dated ever saw was her money and her name.

Were Sebastian any other man, she wouldn't have turned him down. She was young, successful, and in control of her own love life. When she wanted to spend the night with a man, she did, but she chose her lovers carefully. Though she had to admit, these days, the notion had lost its appeal. She craved something more than fleeting. In her heart of hearts, she yearned for something lasting. And Sebastian would never be that man.

She wouldn't be one of his groupies, either. "I won't be another notch on your bedpost, Baz. You and I have known each other for far too long for me to be another body to warm your bed."

Okay, so that was a lie. She knew damn well if he asked, if he didn't stop this torture soon, she'd melt to his whim and beg him to fuck her until she couldn't walk anymore. She'd relish the exchange, too, and to hell with the pain it would leave behind.

She had to say the words, though, because if she ever gave in to the gut-wrenching desire, she'd lose her heart to him. She was already halfway there.

Sebastian didn't seem to be listening. Rather, he trailed his lips up the side of her neck, planting soft openmouthed kisses along the way and leaving goose bumps in his wake. "I have to bury my father in two days and decide if I want to cave to his demands one more time, and it's eating me alive, and you would be a delicious distraction."

She shook her head, desperate to focus. "What demands?"

He let out a bitter, sardonic laugh against her skin. "According to his lawyer, my father left his company to me, but with conditions. In order to save the company *I* built from the ground up when he abandoned it after my mother left, I have to get married. Married! Can you believe that? The bastard."

She furrowed her brow. He wasn't making sense, and he wasn't acting like himself at all. "Have you been drinking, Sebastian?"

He drew back, irritation and offense flaring in his gaze.

"Do you smell liquor on me? No. It's been a long couple of days." He bent his head again, following the curve of her jaw this time. When he reached her ear, he flicked his tongue against the lobe and groaned, low in the back of his throat. "What I need, Tina, is to lose myself in the sweet scent of a woman's body, and you smell positively edible."

Christina's breathing hitched and her core throbbed. Lord help her. He was so damn intense. How the hell did she say no when she craved the exact same thing? His smile alone could make her cream her panties. Her only saving grace was remembering this was out of the ordinary even for him. Sebastian had never looked at her as anything more than Caden's sister, let alone touched her like a woman. Clearly, this was the grief talking.

He sucked her earlobe into his mouth and bit softly. "Say my name."

She swallowed a groan. Her resolve slipped another

notch, and the word left her mouth on a bare whisper. "Baz."

"Wrong one." He rocked his hips into hers, his erection sliding against the softness of her stomach. "Say my name, Tina."

The sound of her pet name on his lips sent a shudder sweeping the length of her spine. She gasped. Her traitorous hands sought out the warmth of his body, sliding up his delicious chest and over the pecs she'd admired only a few minutes ago. His skin was far better than she'd expected. Hotter, sleeker. He had the right amount of chest hair, a light dusting, and the hairs were course yet downy beneath her fingers. The last of her resolve to push him away went up in a puff of good intentions.

His name rolled off her tongue on a defeated sigh. "Sebastian."

His lips trailed the side of her neck, licking, sucking, and nibbling. His hands wandered down her sides to her ass, and he gave her cheeks an appreciative squeeze. "God, you have the finest ass I've ever seen. Say my name again, sweetheart."

"Sebastian." This time she couldn't help herself. His name flew off the tip of her tongue on a quiet whimper. He was gaining ground, and she couldn't do a damn thing to stop him. Truth was, she had no desire to. His mouth on her skin was a fantasy come to life, his hands like heaven. He had complete control over her, and he knew it. Damn him.

He groaned in her ear, a sound of torment and needs denied that had the same firing through her body. His warm palm curved around her left breast, his thumb stroking the elongated, painfully tight nipple. "I love the sound of my name on your lips. God, I ache to hear you moan it when I slide into you."

Oh, for sure he tormented her on purpose, teased her until she melted to his whim. Sebastian liked to toy, to play games, but her body melted regardless. She sagged back against the counter behind her, two desperate little seconds from begging him to do everything he'd said and then some. "Sebastian, please."

This time, his mouth paused on her neck. Seconds ticked out, and her body sat poised, waiting for him to make the next move. She couldn't be certain anymore if she wanted him to stop or continue, but her panties were drenched and her clit throbbed.

Finally, he pinched her left nipple, a delicious combination of pleasure and pain, and pulled back. His eyes blazed at her, the wild look in the depths one part challenge, one part hunger, and one part something she couldn't quite reach. The hunger left her caught for a moment and stole the breath from her lungs. Sebastian had never looked at her that way before.

Before she could form a more coherent thought, he kissed her again, hard, then released her and shoved her away from him.

"You should go. Because if you don't leave right now, I'm going to pick you up and carry you back to my bed, and I'm going to fuck you until you scream my name." He spat the words at her like a threat, pivoted, and stalked away from her.

Christina stumbled back a step. For a moment, she could

only blink and watch his progress. Confusion waged a war in her head. In that moment, she knew two things. He could have had her if he'd wanted her. For a long time, she'd yearned for a single night with him. Just one. A fantasy realized. She'd have gladly given in to his whim, for the pleasure she'd have at his hands, and damn the consequences.

Bigger than that, though, he wasn't himself.

He stopped at the front windows and stood, unmoving, staring out over the city. His shoulders remained stiff, his back straight as a steel rod. Tension radiated off him. As her breathing calmed, a memory floated through her mind. He'd done this before, deliberately pushed her buttons. When Sebastian didn't want to face something, he could evade like nobody's business.

Once when they were kids, he'd pushed until she'd become so angry she'd sworn never to speak to him again. She'd never forget it. They were in fifth grade and she'd been working on her class science project when Sebastian had marched up and told her how stupid he thought her idea was. At that moment, she'd vowed never to speak to him again. Later on, she discovered he'd had a fight with his dad over how much time he'd been spending with her and Caden and not on his studies. Caden had suggested that Sebastian had likely taken his mood out on her. Rather than asking for what he needed—support and kindness—he pushed away the people he held closest to him. Sebastian was used to the people he loved leaving him. First his mother, then his father.

Ever since, she always forgave him, because she knew,

deep down, Sebastian wasn't this man. This was his coping mechanism. Besides, he was family. Did he really think she wouldn't see through him now?

Yes, that's exactly what happened here. He attempted to evade grief, and he'd lashed out at the first person within reach. Oh, for sure he needed someone, but not in the way he'd stated. She'd call Caden later. Being a Monday morning, he and Hannah were no doubt sitting down to breakfast. They were barely a year into their marriage, still newlyweds, and she hated disturbing them. Not to mention Hannah was six months into her first pregnancy. They'd get enough interruptions when the baby came. For now, Sebastian would have to make do with her, because no way would she leave him alone. Clearly, he'd gone down a dark road.

Decision made, she turned to the counter behind her, picked up her purse, and pulled out her cell phone. Then she dialed her assistant's cell. Next month's software release was slightly behind schedule, but she'd have to trust her people to make sure things were getting done. Today, family had to come first. "Hi, Paula. It's Christina. Would you clear my schedule for today, please? We've had a family emergency, and I'm going to need to take the day off. Give my apologies, will you, please?"

"Of course, Miss McKenzie. Is everything all right?" The compassionate worry etching Paula's tone immediately soothed a frazzled nerve. Paula wasn't the most capable assistant she'd ever had. She was a bit clumsy and unsure of herself, but she did anything Christina asked with a bright smile. Now Christina was grateful for her sweet nature.

She sighed and glanced at Sebastian, who continued to stare out the living room windows. "I'm afraid we've had a death in the family. I'm needed at home."

Paula gasped. "Oh no. I'm so sorry, ma'am. My condolences to you and your family. I'll make sure you won't be disturbed."

"Thank you, Paula. I'll try to check in later."

She hung up her phone and returned it to her to purse. Then she toed off her heels and carried them to the edge of the hallway, where she wouldn't trip over them. On her return to the kitchen, she came up short. Sebastian now stood in the kitchen entrance, blocking her path, arms crossed and a firm scowl puckering his brow. "What are you doing?"

She stuck her chin out and pulled her shoulders back. That look meant only one thing: He was about to attempt to intimidate her again. "I'm taking care of you, that's what."

His jaw tightened. "I'm not a child, Tina."

Ignoring his clear attempt to push her off, she pivoted and moved around him, heading around the center island toward the fridge. Thankfully, Lupe kept it well stocked. What Sebastian needed was a friend and a full stomach. In her experience, men were simple creatures. She'd learned by growing up with Caden and her father that the way to tame a riled male usually started with a good meal, so she'd start by making Sebastian breakfast.

She pulled open the refrigerator door and peered inside, ignoring the gaze burning a hole into the back of her head. "It's Chris, if you don't mind, or Christina if you prefer. I'm not ten years old anymore, either, and I know darn well you're aware of that, because you just had your hands all over the proof. I'm staying. You can grump all you want, but don't bother attempting to bully me. I'm not one of your employees or one of your groupies. In case you've forgotten, I graduated from MIT at the top of my class. That means I'm smart, and I'm used to men like you who think they can push me around. You're stuck with me for the morning, Sebastian, so deal with it."

Chapter Two

Sebastian stood at the edge of the kitchen, dumbfounded, watching Christina move about the space like she owned it. His irritation mixed with the lust that still burned through his blood. Before he could utter a word of protest, she pulled a carton of eggs from the fridge, along with shredded cheese and orange juice. The efficiency with which she moved about his kitchen frankly surprised the hell out of him.

He'd been attempting to get her to leave. Of all the days for her to show up, today he actually needed her. He needed her softness, her strength, and God help him, he needed that irritating side of her that insisted on taking care of him. And there she was, making him breakfast. It didn't help that she looked like she belonged in his kitchen.

He drew a calming breath and chose to focus on the mundane details or he'd be taking her back in his arms. He'd gone and done far too much already this morning. "How the hell do you even know how to cook? Don't you have servants who do that?"

She'd grown up in a mansion, the same as he had, with servants who did everything for her, including making her meals and cleaning her room. Hell, if he didn't have Lupe, he'd be eating takeout every night. Yet Christina opened another cabinet, pulled out a large glass bowl and began cracking eggs into it. One-handed.

She tossed a laugh over her shoulder, the sound so light and musical it lit up his insides. In seconds flat, the irritation he'd tried so hard to hold on to flitted from his grasp. He couldn't get the taste of her out of his brain or forget the way she'd pushed herself into his arms.

Damn it all to hell. He dragged a hand through his hair. He hadn't meant to kiss her. He *shouldn't* have kissed her. She was Cade's sister, for crying out loud. That had always made her off-limits. Never mind that he could never give her what she deserved—forever. Christina was important. She and Caden were the only family he had left now. Which meant whatever he felt for her had to be squashed.

Or so he'd always told himself. The problem was, Christina had done what she did best: She'd stood up to him. Damned if her spunk wasn't the sexiest thing about her and he'd fucking caved to his desires like he had no self-control at all.

All kissing her had accomplished was to take his carefully erected walls, ones meant to keep her where he knew he could never lose her, and obliterated them.

Yet there she was, taking over his kitchen like she belonged in it. She had his head filling with visions. Of *her*, in his house, in his life, on a permanent basis. He wasn't sure that life was meant for him. Hell, what he'd done to Jean had proven that. But right then? Christ, he wanted it.

"You're a spoiled brat, Baz. Our cook, Mrs. Humphreys, taught me. You remember her, don't you? She died a couple of years ago. Growing up, whenever I got bored, I'd go hang out in the kitchen with her." As she ducked into a low cabinet to pull out a small frying pan—how she'd known Lupe kept the cookware there, he had no idea—she darted a glance over her shoulder. She arched a brow, that motherly look pinning him to his spot. "I'm assuming by your grouchiness that you haven't eaten this morning? You get crabby when you're tired or hungry."

And aroused, which he was. He was hard enough to hammer nails, because he couldn't forget the luscious press of her nipples against his chest.

His stomach tightened. Christina was a double-edged sword. He loved and hated with equal measure how well she knew him. Despite what he'd told her, he hadn't been sleeping. He'd been lying in bed, staring at the ceiling since he'd gotten home from his father's lawyer's office an hour before. He'd been wishing Christina would show up and do what she did best. Namely, march her way into his apartment and mother hen him to death. Somehow, whenever she did, the care gave him a sense of completeness. It filled a need in his chest he'd been trying to deny for years. The need for a connection, a real connection, to one other person, and not the meaningless flings he'd sworn to himself once satisfied him.

Christina was one of the few people in his life who wasn't paid to do things like this. He'd grown up with nannies and housekeepers, because his father was usually too busy with the resorts, with his women, to do much more than remind him what a constant disappoint he was. He dated unavailable women on purpose: because at the end of the day, it meant no connections. He'd seen firsthand what marriage and love did to a man. His father hadn't been the same since his mother walked out on them twenty years ago.

More to the point, Christina did it because she cared, and it called to the deepest part of him. The part of him that had been in love with her since somewhere around college. And here she was, like a damn domestic goddess.

It didn't help any that she'd chosen one of her pencil skirts this morning. God bless the man who'd developed the pencil skirt. Christina wore them often and she rocked them. This morning's was simple black. The garment hugged her every blessed curve, outlining the subtle flare of her slender hips and her tight little ass. He wanted to shove that skirt to her waist and sink into her warmth. He wanted to make love to her on the counter where she cracked eggs. Then maybe in the shower or the two-person tub in the master bathroom. Or any combination of all three.

Any other time, he relegated his desire for her to other projects. In work. In running. Hell, in other women. This morning, his emotions were raw, all of them on the surface and uncontrollable. He was mad as hell, but the grief was crushing him. His father was the only family he had. His mother's loss was a wound in his chest that would never heal.

He had good and bad memories of her. The smell of her perfume when she hugged him good night. The sound of her laughter, the rare times he'd actually heard her laugh. He also remembered the pain in her eyes and the seemingly constant anger between her and his father. Now he'd lost the only parent remaining, leaving him well and truly alone.

Of all days for Christina to show up, it had to be today. He flat out didn't have the strength to resist her. For a second there, he hadn't been sure he'd be able to stop himself from taking her right in the goddamn kitchen, and all because she'd melted beneath the force of his kiss.

He stifled a miserable groan. Fuck, he hadn't expected that. He'd expected her to slap him and walk out. Hell, he'd have deserved it. Treating her like that was the asshole thing to do for sure, but if he didn't, he'd cave. Again.

"I'll take your silence to mean you haven't eaten yet." Christina glanced at him again. Now busy whisking the eggs, she scowled at him and dumped them into the heated pan, filling the silence with the sound of sizzling. Then she set the bowl into the sink and pointed at the breakfast bar. "Sit."

He glared at her but refused to budge. Damn it. She was the only one, the only woman who got to him, who made him want to confess his every damn secret. "You're bossy, you know that?"

God help him, she was sexy doing that, too. She often stuck her nose in where nobody asked her to, but she always did so with good intentions. She had one of the biggest hearts of any woman he'd ever known.

"I'm not hungry. I'm going for a run." He hated being

rude to her. She didn't deserve it. But if he didn't get out of the house and now, he'd be crossing the kitchen and taking her back in his arms. The way she'd responded to him had stoked the flame in his gut to a full-body burn.

She was too important. If he did any of that, he'd lose her, and if he ever lost her... The thought made his gut ache. So he pivoted and strode toward his bedroom in search of a shirt and his running shoes. He was too damn tired for a run but too keyed up to sleep. Maybe the exercise would finally wear him out.

Christina shot a worried frown over her shoulder. "You have to eat, Baz."

"Later." Sebastian waved a hand behind him, rounded the corner, and shut his bedroom door, closing off the sweet sound of her voice. Two minutes later, he was dressed and striding for the front door. He'd have to remember to buy new shoes. His Nikes were getting worn out.

As he passed the kitchen, Christina shot him a puzzled frown. She stood at the sink, wrists deep in suds. "When will you be back?"

Hand on the doorknob, Sebastian halted. He clenched his teeth, determined not to turn around. Did she have any idea how much she looked and sounded like a wife right then? The thought did nothing for the tangled knot in his gut. She was the only woman he could've ever seen himself with. He'd decided a long time ago marriage wasn't for him, but if ever he wanted to settle down, it would be with her.

"About an hour." He pulled the door open and strode through, letting it fall shut behind him.

* * *

Six miles and forty-five minutes later, he was drenched from a mixture of sweat and rain. As usual for early spring in Seattle, the day was dreary and a sudden shower had opened up on him halfway around the city. Now the muscles in his legs had tightened, because he hadn't stretched before he left, and the endorphins had kicked in, but the run hadn't done a damn thing for the emotion still tangled in his chest. He was wide awake now, but still as stuck as he'd been an hour ago. His father was still dead, and he still had to figure out how to grieve for a man he didn't know if he'd liked. A man he was positive hadn't liked him.

To top it off, he still needed a wife. Of all the stipulations for his father to set. He could still hear the old man's rant. They'd had the same argument at Christmastime last year. *"It's time to grow up, Sebastian."*

His only rebellion was his love life. He'd date who he wanted, when he wanted.

Entering his condo, he came to an abrupt halt at the end of the entry hallway. Christina sat at the breakfast bar, her phone in one hand, a cup of coffee in the other. She'd hooked her feet on the bottom rung of the stool and crossed one endless leg over the other. Her skirt had risen up, giving him a spectacular view of the length of her sleek, taut thighs.

"I'll call you back, Paula. Thanks for your help." She punched a button on her phone and turned to smile at him as she set it on the counter in front of her. "Feel better?"

Did he? For that singular moment in time, her warm

smile shot a dose of sunshine straight into his heart. She had eyes the color of the evergreen trees the state was named for, so bright and luminous he forgot why he ought to be irritated with her. He could get lost in those eyes.

If he could only stop staring at her legs. At five foot ten, Christina was tall for a woman, and her legs seemed to go on forever. He couldn't stop imagining hiking up her skirt, following the length of those legs, and discovering the treasure trove between her luscious thighs. Thinking about it had his cock hardening again. She was so damned beautiful when she smiled at him. He could almost imagine he could have her.

Shit. Apparently he'd be taking a cold shower this morning.

He shot her a scowl as he strode past her, heading for his bedroom. "No. There's an annoying brunette in my kitchen who won't take a hint."

As he passed, her bright smile dropped from her face. "I'm just trying to help, Baz."

Regret tightened in his chest. *Good going. Prove to her yet again that you're just an asshole.*

He paused halfway to his bedroom, caught in indecision, his gut twisting itself into knots. He loathed hurting her, but if he stopped, he was dead. If he turned around, she'd get one hell of a view. He had a tent for crying out loud.

"I need a shower." He muttered the words, then strode for his bedroom, ripping off his clothing and scattering the floor with it on his way to the connected bathroom.

In the shower five minutes later, he turned the water to

the coldest he could stand, but Christina's kiss refused to leave his mind and the longer he stood beneath the water, the harder he became. He couldn't forget the heady flavor of her mouth or the softness of her tongue stroking his. Christ, he had a weakness for tongue kissing, and Christina had it down to a science. The way she'd stroked the insides of his mouth made his cock twitch.

Still impossibly hard, Sebastian banged his head against the cool shower wall and gave in to the need. He grabbed the bar of soap and lathered his hands, then fisted his cock. He needed to ease the ache or he'd be hard all day. Thoughts of Christina wrapped around him like a lure, and he let himself get lost in them. The taste of her hot breath mingling with his. Her lush tits pushing into his chest, her nipples diamond hard. He yearned to know the delicious friction of them rubbing his bare skin as he pounded into her.

Mouth hanging open, breaths coming harsh and ragged, he rocked his hips into his hand. The sweet friction was delicious but not enough. Christina had roused his desire like no other woman could, and he ached for her and her alone. So he closed his eyes and envisioned burying himself deep inside of her. Her long legs wrapped around his hips. Her wet heat milking him for all he had.

The sound of her moaning his name an hour earlier filled his head, and his orgasm rushed up on him, blinding and hot. He held his breath to keep her name from leaving his lips on a desperate groan.

When he emerged from his bedroom forty minutes later, Christina waited for him in the hallway. She leaned against the wall beside his door, arms folded—which did nothing but push her breasts higher.

Sebastian stopped short, his heart hammering. "How long have you been standing there?"

More to the point, had she heard him in the shower?

"Long enough to know you take really long showers." Her eyes narrowed, shooting daggers at him. "You have to be the most infuriating man I've ever known, do you know that? I'm not leaving until I know you'll be okay, because like it or not, I care about you. Caden will be here at noon. Until then, you're stuck with me."

She grabbed him by the wrist, pivoted, and marched into the kitchen. Too surprised and aroused by her outburst to argue, he could only manage to follow the sashay of her ass. Yeah, he loved this side of her. She wasn't afraid of him, wasn't afraid to push back.

Once in the kitchen, she released him and pointed a stern finger at the stool. "Now sit down and eat or so help me God I'll tie you to a chair in the dining room."

The corners of his mouth twitched. Damn it, he couldn't help it. He was half tempted to refuse in order to see her do it. He wasn't into BDSM, but he might be persuaded to try if he knew she'd be the one tying him up.

"Fine." He chose to sit instead, because the food smelled delicious, and his stomach protested loudly. Besides, he'd done enough to her for one day. She stood beside him like a pissed off mama bear, hovering and studying his every move, no doubt because she really was worried. She'd gone through the trouble to cook. The least he could do was eat.

One bite into the omelet she'd made had him groaning with delight. "God, this is good."

She'd made him potatoes, too, tender on the inside, crisp on the outside. The eggs were light and fluffy and cheesy. Exactly the way he liked his breakfast.

"When was the last time you ate, Baz?"

He darted a glance at her as he took a couple swallows of the orange juice on the counter. The expression on her face caught him. She looked relieved. The anger from before had gone. Instead, anxiousness creased her brow.

"I can't help it. I worry about you." She laid a hand against his shoulder, her palm warm through the material of his T-shirt.

His shoulders slumped, his gut sinking into his toes. How the hell did she expect him to resist her when she met his every attempt to push her off with that sweet smile?

He couldn't. Damn it.

"I don't know. Sometime yesterday. I skipped dinner in favor of paperwork when the hospital called." He released a heavy sigh. "I really don't deserve you being this nice to me. I've been a jerk. I'm sorry."

Because I need you too much. The words caught on the tip of his tongue, but Sebastian swallowed them down. Needing distance, lest he tell her all that and then some, he abandoned breakfast and slid off the stool, making his way into the living room. He stopped at the floor-to-ceiling windows that made up the far wall. He'd bought this place for this reason alone: the beautiful view of Elliott Bay. He'd spend hours here, mulling over the day's problems, but today, the view did nothing to soothe his stress.

Christina made him want too much, and his father's stipulations meant he had to marry or forfeit the company he'd spent his adult life building. He had no intention of complying, but no idea either how the hell he'd get his company back. He'd have to talk to his lawyer.

"Today I'll give you a pass."

Her voice sounded behind him, full of quiet amusement and gentle sympathy. Why she always met him with her sweet disposition, he didn't know. He didn't deserve her.

He tossed a smile over his shoulder. "Well, I appreciate it."

He meant that. More than he could possibly tell her.

Christina followed him into the living room, coming to stand behind him. "You don't have to do this alone, Baz."

The pain rose over him, constricting his chest. Her soft concern did what it always did—made him want to confide in her. Some part of his brain told him not to say the words, but as he moved to the sofa and sank, they tumbled from his mouth, unbidden. She was right. He didn't want to be alone, and her caring heart called to the part of him that needed it. "I have so many regrets and so much anger. My whole life was about pleasing him. All I ever wanted was for him to tell me he was proud of me, to tell me he loved me, and he couldn't. Because I reminded him of her. Nothing was ever good enough."

He'd spent his life being his father's greatest disappointment. He'd graduated from Harvard's school of business at the top of his class, had earned his MBA in a year and three months, because he'd worked his ass off for it. Never mind that his father had all but given up on the resorts and *he'd* been the one to take the company worldwide.

"Have they read the will yet?" Christina followed, taking a seat beside him.

Her soft perfume swirled around him like a lure, something subtle and flowery and feminine. Her body heat called to him. It was all he could do not to lean over and inhale the clean, feminine scent of her hair. "I met with my father's lawyer early this morning. My father had everything taken care of. It's the way he handled everything, including dealing with me."

"What happened?"

He shook his head, bile rising with the anger in his stomach. "Gwen, his twenty-five-year-old wife, gets everything. She gets his entire estate, though the money gets divided between us. The hotels and resorts are mine on one condition. I have three months to find a wife, and I have to stay married for a year. If I don't comply, the company reverts to her, the surviving spouse. I'm allowed to keep my job as CEO, but the company will be hers, to do with as she sees fit."

"Meaning, she quite literally gets everything. Baz, I'm sorry." She stared for a moment, eyes searching, conflicted, then slid an arm around him, gathering him closer, and he went, leaning into her in turn. He ought to put a stop to this, get up, go back to bed, but right then, she was everything he needed: kind and compassionate and soothing.

She leaned back on the sofa, pulling him with her, and he lay down beside her, resting his head in her lap. Long moments passed in comfortable silence. Her slender fingers, with her perfectly manicured nails, slid across his scalp over and over, a comforting rhythm as she stroked through his hair. She petted him like a child, or perhaps someone she cared about. Nobody had touched him like this in a long time. Christina's touched soothed the ache inside, and the last of his resistance melted.

"Will you stay?" The words slid off his tongue on a hoarse whisper, and as he waited for her reply, vulnerability rose over him. She had pieces of him he'd never shared with anyone else, and he wasn't certain she knew it. Wasn't certain he could ever tell her or allow the feelings to develop. For today, though, she was here, and he couldn't resist her anymore.

She smoothed his hair back off his forehead. "I'll stay."

* * *

Christina came awake with a start. Forgetting where she was for a moment, she blinked up at the cathedral ceiling. The room around her was quiet, save the soft breathing in her ear. The warm breaths against her neck and the heat of a body against her side had the day rushing back at her. She was still at Sebastian's.

She turned her head, peering at his face. Eyes closed, features slack, he looked like he hadn't a care in the world. He held her tightly to him, and Christina smiled, wistfulness rising over her. After he'd laid his head in her lap, they'd sat in silence for quite a while. He hadn't gotten up, and she hadn't pushed him to. She didn't have anywhere to be today, and when he'd fallen asleep, she'd shifted to lie beside him. He'd gathered her to him, wrapping his arms so tightly around her she could feel his every heartbeat.

Her chest ached for him. Sebastian wasn't a talker. He was a physical person. His diversions appeared to be physical as well. Running. Women. His father's death had obviously left him a place he didn't know how to handle.

As narrow as the sofa was, they'd become entangled in each other as they slept. He'd flung his left arm over her stomach and one heavy leg lay between both of hers, pinning her. Spike had curled up at their feet, in a corner of the sofa, warming her ankles.

Sebastian had buried his face in her neck, and his warm breaths teased her skin. Every puff sent shivers down her spine. If she was honest with herself, she reveled in the strength of his embrace, in the solid warmth of him. Even the way their bodies fit together. She'd long wondered what this would feel like, to lie within the shelter of his arms. Like a lover. It surprised her now natural it felt, like taking a breath, as if they'd done this for years. Nobody had held her like this in a while, either, and she needed him the way he appeared to need her.

He shifted in his sleep, burrowing his face deeper into her throat. When he began to nuzzle her skin, his soft lips skimming her neck, her heartbeat ratcheted up a notch. No doubt he was dreaming, but she couldn't bring herself to stop him. The more logical side of her brain warned that she was heading into dangerous territory, but his soft lips on her skin were irresistible. How many times had she imagined exactly this? Him holding her, kissing her, telling her he wanted her. How many times had she fantasized about being with him?

He moaned in his sleep, a quiet little *hmm* against her throat, and pulled her impossibly tighter against him. His hips rocked forward, his solid erection sliding against her thigh.

Desire curled through her, and she rolled toward him, gathered him closer and let him do what he wanted. To allow herself the luxury of reveling in his touch was taking advantage for sure. He was asleep, no doubt dreaming about some other woman, but far too many months had passed since a man's hands had touched her so intimately. That the touch was Sebastian's provided a lure she couldn't resist.

Oh, she'd had her fair share of one-night stands. They came with her name and her title. Her software development company had done well. She was a computer geek, a programmer at heart, but her success meant she'd met a few gold diggers in her life. Men appeared to see her as a means to line their pockets or their beds or even as a way into her father's good graces. She'd met more than a few who were intimidated by her high IQ.

She'd given up ever finding Mr. Right and had settled for Mr. Right Now. Until Craig. She'd met him three years ago. He'd made her fall in love with him, asked her to marry him and flew her out to Vegas to elope. Turned out, Craig was a playboy, and he'd mixed up his dates, because another woman had shown up that day. She and the woman had sat and talked and laughed, both waiting for their lovers to arrive. Until Craig showed up and they'd both gone to greet him. She'd never forget the look on his face. He'd been caught and he knew it. She'd fled and hadn't seen him again since.

From that day forward, she'd gone into relationships with her eyes wide open, determined never to play the fool again. Sebastian, however, was the one man who held her heart in his hands. He reminded her how much she craved something real. Never mind that he slept, unaware of himself or his actions. To touch him, to encourage his stroking, was invasive at best.

She couldn't deny she wanted him, though. How often over the years had he starred in her erotic fantasies? How many orgasms had she had while imagining his hands and his mouth on her body? And here he was, doing exactly that, after all those scorching kisses in the kitchen earlier. She could only be so strong. God help her, her hips arched against his, her clit throbbing to the pulse of her hammering heartbeat.

Sebastian's eyes fluttered open, sleepy and heavy-lidded. For a moment, he blinked, staring at her, as if trying to remember where he was. Nose to nose now, taking every breath with him, all she could do was wait. She couldn't move for fear she'd beg him to continue. Or worse, that he'd deny her. If he denied her, pushed her away like he had earlier, dismissed her the way he usually did, it would tear her up inside. She needed this tiny connection to him, however wrong it was to want it.

Finally, recognition dawned in his eyes and the arm holding her pinned against his body relaxed. He scooted away from her as much as the space would allow, setting inches between them that felt like miles. "I'm sorry. I was dreaming."

Christina watched him for a moment, heart hammering her breastbone. She'd always promised herself if the moment ever presented itself, she'd never give in to him, but his kisses and erotic touches earlier had worn down her defenses. The voice of reason screamed in her head to stop. *Remember Craig?*

The question rose on her tongue all the same. Putting it out there was a flat-out risk, but she had to know the answer. It had burned a hole in her brain for hours. "Why'd you kiss me earlier?"

His eyes searched her face, a war waging in the depths. Confusion. Indecision. "I shouldn't have."

Christina held her breath. "But why did you?"

He was silent a moment before releasing a heavy sigh. His touch slow and tentative, he stroked a finger along her cheekbone and across her jaw. "Because you caught me in a weak moment. I'm sorry. I was craving a distraction, and you were in the line of fire."

His words lodged themselves inside of her and stuck there, taunting her with what she wanted so badly she ached with it. Because along with his earlier kisses, his quiet admission hinted that maybe, just maybe, he really did see her as more than Caden's sister. It didn't help that he stroked a thumb across her bottom lip with all the familiarity of a tender lover, and her mind took the moment and ran with it. If all she got was one night, wouldn't it be worth it? A chance to fulfill the fantasy? She could handle one night…couldn't she?

Not giving herself time to overthink her impulsive decision, Christina pressed along his length. Their clothing did little to separate them, and his thick erection throbbed against her stomach, a luscious lure. Despite the uncertainty and vulnerability rising in his eyes, one hand slid over the curve of her hip and smoothed down over her ass. His palm warmed her backside through the thin fabric of her skirt.

She lifted trembling fingers and sifted them through his hair. Never in all the time she'd known him had she ever been so bold before. She couldn't stop shaking. "And if I offered to be that distraction?"

She *hoped* he'd gather her closer and kiss her back. Kiss her the way he had earlier in the kitchen, though if he accepted, anything more would have to wait. Caden was due soon. But the need to know his response beat behind her breastbone like the hammering of her pulse.

Instead, regret rose in his eyes. He shook his head and sat up, effectively shutting her out as he moved to take a seat on the edge of the sofa.

He set his feet on the floor, his body stiff beside her. "I appreciate the sentiment, Tina, I really do, but I can't."

For a moment, she couldn't move, couldn't breathe, as she processed his words. As his rejection finally sank in, hurt and disappointment reverberated through her chest. Heat flooded her face. How utterly embarrassing. Of course he wouldn't see her as anything other than Caden's sister. And here she was, throwing herself at him.

"Oh gosh. I'm so sorry." Numb from head to toe, she nodded and sat upright. As she straightened her skirt, she forced a laugh, hoping somehow to save face. She'd never done that before. She'd always been the geek, the smart girl, and she'd never gone for unobtainable men. Like him. "Clearly I read you wrong. Forgive me. I assumed you needed *me* when you kissed me, but you didn't. I was just a warm body, a momentary distraction, and one you clearly regret. I'll be out of your hair. I've imposed enough. Caden will be over soon."

She returned her laptop into the bag leaning against the end table leg, where she'd left it while Sebastian went for a run, then stood and looped the bag over her right shoulder. Behind her, Sebastian went silent, but his gaze burned into her as she made her way into the kitchen. She stuffed her cell phone into her purse and pivoted, heading for her shoes at the end of the hallway.

Sebastian let out a quiet laugh behind her that was half miserable groan. "God, I can't believe you haven't figured it out yet."

She stopped at the end of the hallway, torn by indecision. She *needed* to leave, before her heart cracked in two pieces. The desire to know, however, won out.

"Figured out what?" She folded her arms over her stomach, clutching her purse to her and using it as a lifeline.

"How I feel about you."

Christina froze, her heart pounding. He spoke softly, with reluctance, but once again he skirted around the issue, answering her question without really answering. So far this morning, he'd kissed her, attempted to seduce her, then when she'd offered herself to him, he'd turned *her* down. Suddenly she was supposed to understand what the hell he was talking about?

His subtle comment also hinted once again that he cared for her, and the tease was one too many. Her last nerve snapped, and she pivoted to face him. Frustrated tears welled in her eyes, but she blinked them back and swallowed past the knot in her throat. "How am I supposed to know how you feel about me when you treat me like Caden's annoying little sister? Like you can barely stand the sight of me? I don't know whether I'm coming or going this morning."

She threw her hands in the air and met his bewildered stare with a glare. Once out, the words erupted from her lips, unstoppable.

"I'm in love with you. Did you know that? I've *been* in love with you for so long I can't remember when I fell. I think it was somewhere in high school, when you decked Bobby Stalwart. Do you remember that? I do. I'll never forget. He'd cornered me against a locker, put his hands all over me, taunted me. He asked me if my intelligence meant I was good in bed, too, and you marched over and broke his nose."

Sebastian had gotten in the football star's face and told Bobby if he so much as looked at her the wrong way again, he'd break his throwing arm next time. It was the first time she'd realized Sebastian even gave a damn about her.

Chest heaving and her heart pounding against her rib cage, Christina turned back around, shoved her feet in her heels, and marched toward the front door. For a moment, only the sound of her heels *click-clacking* across the hardwood floor filled the space. Even Spike, who usually walked with her to say goodbye, was nowhere to be found.

Halfway down the hallway, the emotions eating her up refused to be held back, and she turned and marched back into the kitchen. Sebastian, halfway around the couch now, halted as she faced him, eyes wide and stunned.

"By the way, you don't want to participate in the bachelor auction this year? Fan-fucking-tastic. It'll save me from having to watch all your groupies throw themselves at you. Having to sell you like a goddamn pimp, all the while knowing the woman you go home with no doubt gets the privilege of sharing your bed, flat-out sucks."

She didn't bother to wait for his reply but spun and left his condo, slamming the door behind her. What a complete and utter disaster. Well, now she knew the answer to *that* question, didn't she?

Chapter Three

Sebastian dragged his hands through his hair. Heart in his throat, his gut tied in sickening knots, he could only stare at the door. Christina had slammed it so hard the walls rattled. The panic seated in his chest told him to go after her. Even Spike looked ticked at him. *His* cat—his, damn it!—came wandering out from God knew where and took a seat at the end of the hallway. Ears back, tail twitching in irritation, Spike seemed to glare at him. Even Spike's hate-filled look seemed to say, *Go get her, stupid!*

His brain and his common sense, however, said to let her go. He'd wanted to put distance between them, to save her from him, and he'd accomplished the task. In freakin' spades. God, he'd almost caved. Her offer was selfless, but her heart had been in her eyes. She'd have given herself to him because he needed her, but the knowledge filled his mind with impossible questions. Namely, how the hell could he not have noticed that she loved him? He'd never dared allowed himself to dream of the possibility. Her touch had been soft, and the tenderness in her eyes was a lure he'd nearly given in to.

But he refused to use her. Christina would never be a meaningless fling to fill a need, and he wouldn't treat her like one. Her words kept repeating in his mind, though, tormenting him.

"I'm in love with you. Did you know that?"

The look on her face. The pain and shock in her eyes. Christina put out an air of confidence. She was comfortable with who she was, but obviously still had old hurts buried in there somewhere. She was smart. She was right. Men like him usually liked the party girls. He dated girls like that on purpose. They wanted exactly what he did: a good time with no strings attached.

A relationship with Christina meant all kinds of strings. Her brother had been his best friend since first grade, for crying out loud. He'd known her before puberty, before breasts, when she'd been that annoying know-it-all on the playground. She and Cade had been there when his mother left and his parents divorced, and they'd been there during his teenage rebellion. Out of all the people in his life, Cade and Christina were the most important. He'd just gotten his relationship with Cade back on track. Three years ago, he'd gotten himself tangled with a woman who'd used them both, pitting them against each other for financial gain. Amelia's game had nearly cost him his best friend. He wouldn't screw up a good friendship for what amounted to great sex.

Still, the hurt on Christina's face haunted him. He'd put that pain there, and he hated himself for it.

He looked to Spike and shook his head. "How the hell did I manage to screw that up so spectacularly?"

Spike flicked his tail in irritation and turned, sauntering across the floor in the direction of the living room. Once there, he hopped onto his favorite spot on the windowsill and sat looking out over the city. Sebastian's mind churned, going in a million different directions. How did he fix this when he needed Christina so damn much? How did he separate himself from that phenomenal kiss? How the hell did he forget that?

The doorbell sounded, interrupting his musings, and he jerked his gaze to the door. It wouldn't be her. On a logical level, he understood that. Why the hell would she come back? Yet his heart skipped a hopeful beat anyway.

"Cross your toes, Spike." He jogged down the hallway and yanked open the door.

Only to have his heart sink into his toes a moment later. The person on the other side wasn't Christina but Cade. He stood in the vestibule, wearing a full suit, hands tucked in the pockets of his navy slacks.

Sebastian blew out a breath in disappointment. "Oh, it's you."

Cade let out a quiet laugh. "Hi to you, too. What the hell did you do to Chris?" He jerked a thumb over his shoulder. "I met her on the street outside the building. She was hell-bent about something. Told me I should let you rot in hell."

Sebastian closed his eyes, suddenly exhausted. His shoulders slumped with the weight pressing down on him. "I couldn't have screwed that up more if I tried."

"What the hell did you do to make her so mad?"

Sebastian opened one eye, peering at Cade with caution. "I kissed her."

Then he braced himself. This could go one of two ways. He'd never confided his feelings for Christina to Cade. Not officially at least, though he knew Cade wasn't stupid or blind. Cade was a lawyer, and a damned good one. Sebastian was too afraid of getting hit, particularly after the fiasco that was Amelia. He had to be some kind of stupid not to realize the woman who'd seduced him at the bar that night was his best friend's fiancée. She'd had the same name, after all. He'd been elbows deep in a bottle of scotch, hell-bent on getting drunk enough to forget running into Christina and her latest lover.

How protective would Cade be of Christina, though? If you asked him, your best friend's sister should be off-limits, period, and Sebastian didn't have the best track record.

Across the threshold, Cade grinned, ear to freakin' ear.

"About damn time." He stepped over the threshold, closed the door behind him, and hitched a shoulder. "Why's she so pissed?"

Sebastian turned, leading Cade into the kitchen. "She showed up at a bad time, and I blew it in a major way. What else?"

As they came to a stop beside the center island, Cade laid a hand on his back. "She told me about your father. I'm sorry. Is there anything I can do?"

Sebastian let out a harsh laugh. "Yeah. Find a loophole for my father's last dying demand."

At Cade's questioning stare, he related the details of his father's will. By the time he finished, Cade was in stitches.

"Married? You?" Cade shook his head, his voice still shaking with laughter. "One last dig from beyond the grave. Oh, that's a tough one, man."

"Very helpful, bro." Sebastian shot him a glare and moved to the coffeepot on the opposite counter. He grabbed a mug from the overhead cabinet, filled it from the cold coffeepot, and stuck the mug in the microwave, setting it for a minute. He faced Cade again, leaned back against the counter's edge, and folded his arms. "I refuse to go along with it, but how the hell am I going to get past it? Damned if I'm going to just give his wife my company."

"There are probably ways around it, but it might not be easy. I can look into if you want." Cade leaned back against the opposite counter and slipped his hands in his pockets. He arched a brow. "You know, you might consider complying. I'm betting I know a certain brunette who'd marry you simply because you asked, and she wouldn't take a cent of your money. And you can't tell me you haven't thought about it."

The microwave beeped, and Sebastian turned. He shook his head as he opened the door and pulled out his mug.

"First of all, I don't think Tina would give me the time of day right now. I think she'd rather run me over with her BMW, and I'm not sure I'd blame her." He resumed his place against the kitchen counter and sipped his coffee, grateful for the dose of caffeine. "Second of all, I'm not getting married. I'm not marriage material, and besides, I'm positive I'd only make her miserable. She deserves better than someone like me."

Cade shook his head. "I don't agree. I think she's exactly the woman you need and there's nobody I'd trust more with her than you. What the hell did you two fight about, anyway?"

Sebastian lowered his mug, staring for a long moment at Cade. Did he dare tell Cade the truth? Finally, he sighed and grinned, pointing his index finger. "First you have to promise not to hit me."

Cade, however, didn't laugh. Rather, his expression sobered, shoulders rounding to match the dejection and regret washing across his features. "I shouldn't have hit you in the first place. I'm really glad you forgave me for that."

Oh, they'd had it out over Amelia, all right. Sebastian had discovered she wasn't who she'd said when Cade had let himself into her apartment with the key she'd given him. Cade had immediately assumed the worst, and Sebastian had gotten a black eye for his trouble. She'd snowed both of them.

Sebastian offered a smile. "Ditto. It's over and done with. I'm glad to have my best friend back. I missed you, man."

Cade rolled his eyes, but one corner of his mouth hitched. "Save the mush for Chris. So? Spill it. What did you do?"

Sebastian peered at Cade over the rim of his coffee mug as he took a sip. Somehow, he had to soften the blow of this one. "Let's just say things got a little hot and heavy, and I turned her down."

Cade stared for a moment, his expression blank. He blinked. "Wait. You turned *her* down?"

Sebastian moved around the breakfast bar, meandering toward the front windows, lost in memories of this morning. Spike, clearly still pissed at him for making Christina leave, flicked his tail and hopped off the sill, heading for the back bedroom. "I wasn't in a good place when she arrived. I was exhausted, I'd been up all night, and I'd just come back from a visit with my father's lawyer. You know how she is. Barging in and deciding she's going to mother you to death."

Behind him, Cade groaned in commiseration. "I love my sister, but that drives me up the freakin' wall. She stops by every morning on her way to work to make sure I'm giving Hannah what she needs. Like I haven't a damn clue what my own wife needs."

"Exactly. This morning she pushed the wrong button, and I cracked. I told her things I shouldn't have told her, and I touched places I shouldn't have touched."

Cade let out a half laugh, half groan. "Please, for the love of my sanity, do *not* go into detail. There are things I really don't need to know about my sister."

Sebastian chuckled. "We got to talking and one thing led to another. Better?"

"Thank you. And?"

"And she made me an offer no man in his right mind would turn down, but I had to. Because I'm me, and she deserves better. She told me off and stormed out. Apparently, I'm hiding my feelings from her better than I thought. She says I treat her like an annoying kid sister, like I can't stand her."

Cade let out a quiet laugh. "She's right. You're an irritable son of a bitch when she's around."

Because he usually had the hard-on of the century. One glance at her in one of those damn pencil skirts and his cock sprang to attention. When she actually touched him, brushed against him or did something insane like hug him—which she did a lot, because Christina, God love her, was a hugger—it was all he could do to keep from pushing his erection into the softness of her body. Because she was so fucking incredibly baby soft. His biggest fantasy was getting the luxury of rubbing his aching cock against her bare, warm skin.

It was pathetic, and being hard all the damn time made him irritable as hell. He always hoped if he grouched at her, she'd get pissed and leave. Treating someone he cared about that way was horrible, but if he didn't, he always feared he'd crack. Exactly the way he had this morning. He wanted more for her than someone like him.

Sebastian darted a glance behind him. "How *is* Hannah, by the way?"

Cade, now seated on one of the stools at the breakfast bar, smiled, the kind so filled with joy and contentment envy kicked Sebastian hard in the chest. "Hannah's great. She sends her condolences. Morning sickness has been rough. Six months into this pregnancy, and she's still throwing up. Is there anything I can do? Do you need someone to make funeral arrangements?"

Sebastian sipped his coffee. "No, but thanks. Everything's done. Father had everything put into his will years ago. One phone call to his lawyer this morning had all the pieces set into motion within hours." He raised his brows. "Come to the funeral?"

"You know it." Cade flashed a warm smile.

The knot in his gut eased a bit. Cade's support meant a lot. He wouldn't get through the next few days on his own.

"I appreciate it." If ever he'd had a brother, Cade would have been it.

Cade glanced at his watch, rose from his seat, and crossed the space between them, tucking his hands in his pockets. "Listen, I have to get back. I'm sorry to leave so soon, but I've got a meeting with a client in a half hour who couldn't reschedule. Why don't you come over for dinner tonight? I should be home by six. Hannah makes an awesome meat loaf."

Sebastian couldn't help the chuckle that left him. "She's definitely domesticated you. Meat loaf? Seriously?"

"Being domesticated has its perks. You should try it sometime." Cade bumped his shoulder, then sobered a breath later. "Text me with the details about the funeral?"

"Will do. And thanks."

Cade clapped him on the back. "Anytime. Call me if you need anything."

He walked Cade out, then shut the door behind him, and sagged back against it. Cade had a point. He wanted, ached and needed, to straighten out the mess he'd made with Christina. Some part of him yearned for what he'd never have with her, but her happiness mattered, too.

If he got involved with Christina, he'd only end up hurting her the way he had Jean. Jean was on the top of his long list of regrets. He'd met her at the company Christmas party at the resort in L.A. Technically, she worked for him as the branch manager. He'd gone down there because he hated holidays. His father always took his latest wife on some exotic vacation. He and Jean had ended up in bed together two days before Christmas and spent the entire weekend together.

She was the first and last woman he'd really tried with. For years, he'd been determined not to become his father and had gone into a relationship with Jean determined to make it work. Two years in, she'd confessed her love for him. He'd cared about her. A lot. But he didn't love *her*.

When he couldn't say the words back, she'd walked away. He'd hated hurting her, but he wouldn't be that guy who lied just to keep her around.

No, someway, somehow, he'd get around his father's stipulations, but not by getting married.

He turned his head. Across the way, sitting in a corner of the living room, his guitar stood in its stand. He'd picked up playing in junior high. Turned out, he was pretty good at it. He'd played in a band for a while in high school and college, but they broke up after graduation. Life had moved on.

Maybe playing in a band wouldn't have paid the bills. He might not have ended up with a huge record label, touring the world. Hell, he had to admit his father was right on that account. He might not have ended up where he had if he'd followed his dreams, and he was proud of what he'd accomplished. Their small family business wouldn't have ended up on the Fortune 500 list if he hadn't been determined to drive it there.

They were *his* dreams, though, and his father had squashed them. No way in hell was wife number five getting her hands on his company.

He still had no desire to get married, though, and no desire to hurt Christina any more than he already had. She deserved better. This was the best for her, whether he liked it or not.

* * *

Standing with his "stepmother," Gwen, beside his father's casket Wednesday morning, Sebastian attempted to go numb as he listened to the pastor give the sermon. He was determined to get through this damn funeral without feeling much of anything.

The day itself was cool and drizzly, the sky overcast. A blanket of gray blocked out what sun they might have had, but apparently Mother Nature couldn't decide if she wanted it to actually rain. The dismal weather suited his mood. The funeral had a good turnout. Several hundred people had come to pay their respects, but getting through the service had to be one of the hardest moments of his life. Harder even than the day his father had blatantly pointed out that Mom wasn't coming back.

Today, too much emotion had caught in his chest. Regret.

Grief. Anger. He hadn't the foggiest damn idea how to deal
with any of it. There was too much he wished he'd had the
guts to tell the old man when he lived.

Turning his head, he fixed his gaze on Christina's still
form among the gatherers. She stood toward the front with
Cade and Hannah, looking gorgeous in a simple black suit.
She'd greeted him politely at the funeral parlor, as decorum
dictated, but any time he met her gaze, hers filled with a cool
aloofness, not at all as open as she'd been two days ago. He
missed her smile, and he hated the tension between them.

As the pastor said the final prayer, Gwen sobbed quietly
beside him, what looked like big, fat crocodile tears. She and
his father had only known each other for a little more than
a year, three whole months before they married, yet she appeared to be falling to pieces. He didn't buy a single bit of it.

When the service finished, he stood to do his part.
"Thank you all for coming. At the request of the widow, no
gathering will be held."

Too exhausted and too numb for any more, he turned
and negotiated his way through the crowd toward his limo,
parked at the curb. He wanted to go home. He'd taken the
rest of the day off, leaving his assistant with the order to
call him should anything pressing arise. The newest resort
in Milan was supposed to have been completed by now.
He'd hoped the resort would be finished before the summer
season hit, but things never quite went according to plan.
Complications had risen, and he'd have to push the opening
off until June.

For today, though, he was going home and taking a run.

He wanted to run long and hard, to work off the anger and grief and frustration caught in the web of crap in his chest. Then he had plans to get out his guitar. He hadn't played in months. He'd been too busy. Maybe if he did, maybe if he gave in to the pull and let the music soothe his soul the way it used to, he'd actually sleep tonight.

He hadn't slept worth a damn since Christina left his apartment the other day. Oh, she'd been angry with him plenty of times over the years. Hell, he ought to be used to it. This time, something was different. She'd opened a line of honesty between them, and the ache in his gut wouldn't go away. Having to be here, of all places, without her beside him nagged at him as being flat-out wrong. Of all the days for her to mother hen him to death, today was another day he actually needed her.

* * *

Christina followed Sebastian's progress as he wandered away from the gravesite. Shoulders hunched, his expression cool and impassive. Regret mixed with the pain seated in her chest. She'd thrown herself at him and made a fool of herself. His emphatic refusal had stung more than a little.

He'd buried his father this morning, though, and the sight of his carefully masked grief had her heart in a tangle in her chest.

Caden leaned over and nudged her elbow with his hand. When she turned to look at him, he nodded in Sebastian's direction, brow furrowed, gaze stern. Christina braced her-

self. She knew that look. Caden was about to get his lecture
on.

"He won't say it. He'll never ask, but he needs us today.
Whatever beef you have with him, put it away for another
day. Sebastian's family." He took Hannah's hand, tucking it
into the crook of his arm.

Hannah gave her a warm smile, touched her shoulder,
and the two moved in Sebastian's direction. Over the last
six months, Hannah had become a treasured friend. They'd
met initially when Cade and Hannah had first started seeing
each other, though their friendship hadn't officially begun
until the two announced their engagement. Hannah amazed
her. She'd lost her parents in a terrible car accident and wore
the scars of that day—literally. A huge slash cut across her
right cheek, too deep to be hidden by makeup. And while
she grew up fending for herself, not in the luxury Christina
and Caden had, she fit into their family, like she'd been born
into it. She was good for Caden. Christina and Hannah's
business partner, Maddie O'Riley, had become friends during Caden and Hannah's wedding.

Christina turned, following their progress with her eyes.
They greeted Sebastian at the curb, each hugging him tightly
for a moment. Hannah murmured something, and Sebastian
took her hand, gave her a warm but tired smile, and
squeezed her fingers. Caden murmured something in his ear,
and Sebastian nodded before Caden and Hannah moved
off.

Her gut knotted. Caden was right. Sebastian was family.
Were she angry with Caden, she wouldn't have allowed an

argument to keep her from supporting him. Why should it be any different with Sebastian?

With a sigh, she made her way toward him, stopping at the edge of the sidewalk. Another couple she didn't recognize stopped to offer condolences. Every fiber of her body trembled as she waited. Nausea rolled through her stomach. When the older couple moved away, she drew a deep breath, buried her pain and anger, and stepped up beside him. This was about him. Not her.

His scent blew in on the breeze, and her fingers itched to reach out and touch him. Any other time, she'd have wrapped him in a fierce hug, put him in the limo, and taken him home. This time, she kept her hands to herself. She didn't know if she had the right to do that anymore.

Sebastian glanced at her, and the tension between them ramped up several notches. Something she couldn't quite grasp worked in the depths of his eyes.

"Are you all right?" She had so much more she wanted to say to him. It likely wasn't what he needed to hear, but it was the safest thing for both of them.

"I'm fine." He turned to stare out over the roof of the limo and stood silent a moment, hands in the pockets of his black slacks. Finally, he drew a deep breath and blew it out. "I'm sorry I hurt you. It's never intentional. You have to know you get to me."

If at all possible, the tension ramped up another thousand degrees, a wall that erected between them. For the first time since she'd known him, Sebastian had become a stranger. He'd always treated her like a kid sister at worst, a friend at best. This nothingness ate at her. They'd crossed a line they couldn't go back from and it became the Great Wall of China between them.

Sebastian turned his back to her and dragged his hands through his hair, holding it off his forehead the way he did when frustrated. Finally, he dropped his hands, flashing a gentle smile that didn't reach his eyes. The pain in his gaze had her breath catching in her throat and her fingers twitched again with a desperate need to hug the stuffing out of him. Angry or not, he was clearly hurting. Right then, he held the weight of the world on his shoulders, and her heart ached with the need to take some of it from him.

"I'm sorry. I need to get out of here, or I'm going to implode. Thank you for coming. I appreciate the support." He nodded at his driver and climbed inside the limo.

The driver shut the door, leaving her standing on the sidewalk with a hole in her chest. Why did she feel like she'd lost her best friend? And why was she still so damn tempted to follow him into his limo and take him home?

The limo drove off before she'd taken her next breath, leaving her staring after him. A war waged in her chest. She'd have to head back to the office, pretend her head was in the game for the board meeting this afternoon, when everything inside of her, every fiber of muscle and every cell of blood, begged her to go after him. Sebastian Blake had her caught somewhere between here and eternity, and she had no idea which end was up anymore.

* * *

Christina jolted awake. She stared at the dark ceiling above her, watching the play of shadows for a moment, trying to discern what had woken her. The heater ran, blowing warm air through the house, but otherwise, the night was silent. When pounding came from the front door, she turned her head to look at the clock: 1:02 a.m. blinked back at her in bright red numbers.

When the doorbell rang next, she pried herself out of bed, grabbed her robe off the ottoman at the end, and wrapped the garment around her as she padded to the front door. Unlike Caden and Sebastian, Christina owned a small house. She hated apartment living, wedged in on all sides with neighbors, no privacy, noises at all hours of the night. She'd tried it once right after college, had bought a small condo in Clyde Hill. Within six months, she'd realized it wasn't for her.

No, she'd wanted a home, like the one in which she'd grown up. Her small house sat in a neighborhood full of families. Exactly why she'd bought the place. Her neighbors were kind people, and the house was her dream. She wanted what the people surrounding her had. A home and a family.

More to the point, they'd all gone to bed by now. The neighborhood quieted down after dark. Who'd show up on her doorstep at one in the morning? Worry etched her mind. It wouldn't be Caden. If something had happened, he'd have called first. Same with her mother.

The person on the other side pounded again as she undid the locks.

"All right, all right. For crying out loud, I'm…" As she

yanked the door open, the rest of her complaint died in her throat. "Sebastian."

He stood beneath the awning of the front porch in the shirt and slacks he'd worn to the funeral, though he'd lost his jacket and tie. He leaned his hands on the door frame, looking up at the sound of her voice. He didn't give her time to ask what he was doing there so late. Instead, he frowned and stepped inside. He closed the door behind him, took a moment to latch it, then turned to her. Eyes feral and dark, he backed her against the adjacent wall and set his hands on either side of her head, reminiscent of that morning in his condo.

Her heart caught in her throat. Blood flooded every muscle, and her core throbbed. He was so close his scent invaded her nostrils. His cologne, a clean and masculine scent, mixed with the all-male aroma clinging to him and went to her head in a rush. He'd also been drinking. The aroma of alcohol, scotch if she wasn't mistaken, wafted over her as his breath puffed against her lips. She chose to focus on that and not the way the wild look in his heavy lidded eyes made her knees tremble. God, he was sexy when he looked at her like that.

She sagged back against the wall. "You've been drinking."

Sebastian's gaze flicked down her body, and he drew a sharp breath, his nostrils flaring. As he met her gaze again, hunger blazed in his eyes.

"That robe doesn't cover a damn thing. I can see your every curve." His hand came up, his thumb boldly sweeping the tip of her left breast. His voice lowered to a husky murmur. "I can see the shape of your nipples through this thing."

Her nipple tightened in an instant, begging for another stroke of his fingers. She bit the inside of her cheek to stifle a needy gasp and tried one more time to reason with him. "Please tell me you didn't drive over here, Baz."

"I've had three drinks. Granted, they were doubles, but I'm not drunk. Delightfully fuzzy, maybe, but not drunk. I think today warranted a drink. And, no, I didn't drive." One corner of his mouth hitched, and his eyes lit up, playful, childish, and completely Sebastian. "Having more money than God has its perks. I had my driver bring me. The man needs a damn raise for getting out of bed for me at one in the morning."

Christina drew her brows together and shook her head, forcing her mind to focus. "Why are you here? What on earth couldn't wait a few hours?"

He leaned into her, resting his forearms on the wall beside her head. Her breath caught. Oh God. He was so close now his hot breath whispered over her cheek. An inch at most separated them, and every inch of *her* waited on the edge of a precipice for him to make the next move.

"I see you." The words came as a tender murmur between them. He tucked her hair with the tip of his index finger, letting the digit graze the top of her ear.

Hot little shivers raced along the surface of her skin, from the point of contact outward. Instantly recognizing the line from a movie she knew he'd seen because they'd watched it together, Christina attempted to regain her equilibrium and rolled her eyes. Pushing back was her only saving grace at this point. "That's a cheesy line, even for you."

He shook his head, his gaze deadly somber. "No, I mean it. I can't believe we've known each other all this time, and you still haven't a clue how I feel about you. God, sometimes it consumes me. Some days it's all I can do to keep busy enough not to think about it. It always manages to surprise me that you don't seem to see it, because I often feel like I'm made of glass, like you can see right through me."

Her breath caught in her throat, and a desperate ache settled between her thighs. Oh, she hadn't anticipated him saying that. It didn't help that he stroked his finger down her temple, traced the line of her cheek and jaw, the touch soft and tender and leaving goose bumps in its wake. All she could do was remember the in and out of breathing.

"For the record, I was a little surly that morning, because you pushed all my damn buttons and all it did was turn me on. When you get in my face and push back, it always turns me on. It's why I kissed you. I couldn't stand it. Except that kiss left me hard enough to hammer nails. Never in a million years did I expect you to kiss me back. When I took my shower, I had a nice orgasm while imagining my cock buried deep inside of you."

She couldn't stop her eyes from widening or the soft gasp that left her mouth. In two seconds flat, the image filled her mind. Sebastian naked and wet, his cock in his hand. Did he close his eyes when he came? Did he tremble? Cry out? Or groan softly?

Her breathing ramped up, coming now in shallow, desperate pants. Christ. Every single fantasy she'd ever had starring him flooded her thoughts, and a lethal dose of shock and desire zinged through her system. Her clit throbbed in delicious need.

He grinned, as if he could read her mind. "Yeah. Imagine that. While you made me breakfast, I had my cock in my hand. When I came all over the shower wall, your name left my lips."

He ground his hips into hers, his cock hard and throbbing against the softness of her stomach. Apparently not done tormenting her, he bent his head and nipped at the curve of her shoulder, his soft, supple lips skimming the side of her neck.

"Shit, Tina. The feel of your soft body against me while I slept that morning was equal parts blessing and torment. Waking in your arms was a fantasy come to life. Turning you down was the single hardest damn thing I've ever done." He stroked the tips of his fingers down the back of her right arm, his voice lowering to an intimate murmur. "I can't tell you how much it eats me alive to know I hurt you, but, sweetheart, I'm not what you need. You deserve the white picket fence and forever, and I'm not a forever kind of guy. I won't use you that way."

Oh God. He had to say it. Sebastian was letting his walls down, letting her in, and her heart melted and ached simultaneously. Hearing those words from his mouth was a double-edged sword. It hurt to hear them and yet her heart glommed onto one point: He was essentially telling her he saw her. As a woman. As more than Caden's sister.

How long had she craved to hear him tell her that? That he gave a damn? That he'd admitted it meant he really did have a good heart, that she hadn't misjudged him, and she appreciated his honesty. But he was right. He had a heart he refused to give to anyone, her included. In the end, hers would get broken when he walked away from her. Which meant she had to be strong now.

Desperate to hold on to what little sanity she had left, she hiked her chin a notch. Sebastian in seduction mode was a powerful force. To be on the receiving end of all that masculine prowess made her dizzy with need. It was all she could do not to wind her arms around his neck and beg him to make love to her, right there against the wall. "Why are you here? Did you really come to my house at one in the morning to tell me that?"

"I came because I'm weak." He bent his head, skimming his lips up the side of her neck. "I needed you today. You want to know what I see in you? What makes you different from the women I date? What is it you call them? Groupies? Everything about you is soft and feminine. The way you walk, the way you talk. Even shoving your face in mine and poking me in the chest, you're still soft around the edges. It drives me crazy, because it's so fucking…"

He shook his head, growling in frustration.

She bit the inside of her cheek, her back stiffening. If he insulted her or told her once again how much she couldn't have him, she'd clobber him. She really would. "What? Annoying? Irritating?"

His warm breath whispered over her as he brushed the

lightest of kisses across her lips. So tender her breath caught in her throat.

"Sexy. Beautiful. Phenomenal. Take your pick. You're an incredible woman, Tina." He shook his head, his voice lowering to a murmur between them. "I choose the women I spend time with for a purpose. I prefer the party girls. They serve a need in the moment and don't expect anything. Go ahead. Ask me why they're always blondes."

She pursed her lips and glared at him. All she had left was to hold on to the last bit of her anger. "I have no desire to know, Sebastian."

He nipped at her bottom lip, ground his hips into her, rubbing his erection into her belly, and groaned.

"The last brunette I tried to make love to, I spent the entire time fantasizing about you. To the point that I couldn't do it. I sent her home, angry as hell and cussing me a blue streak." He stroked the shell of her ear, a tender stroke. "Because she wasn't you."

Hot little shivers chased each other up and down her spine. Goose bumps prickled her skin, making every hair stand on end. Every nerve ending caught fire, every inch of her alive and throbbing and craving him. His touch. His kiss.

She closed her eyes, shutting out the hunger in his gaze, but couldn't bring herself to push him back. His touch set a blaze inside of her. No man's touch had ever been this good, had ever been so…right. God help her, she needed it. She needed *him*.

She let out a soft, miserable groan on a shuddering breath. The last of her resistance evaporated on a puff of smoke.

"Why are you telling me this? I don't want to know about you and your other women. This is the stuff that kills me, Baz."

"Because you need to know. Because I give up trying to resist you. I don't have the strength today. I buried my father this morning. I gave up every damn dream I had to try and be what he wanted me to be, so one day he'd turn to me and tell me how proud he was of me. And he turned his back on me, not once but twice. That bitch gets everything I worked my life for, because she's got big tits and a tight ass."

His big, warm hands slid down her sides and over the curve of her hips. He pulled her tight against him, buried his face in her throat, and wrapped his arms around her.

"I need you, Tina. I need your softness. I need your strength. I just…need you. Not anybody. You. Always you. Please don't make me go home."

She swallowed past the lump of fear stuck in her throat. God help her heart. He'd done it. He'd said the exact right thing, in a way only he could. Come morning, she'd probably regret sleeping with him, but she didn't have the strength to deny him. He needed her, and like she needed to draw her next breath, she needed him.

She opened her eyes and wrapped her arms around him, then turned her head and skimmed her lips up the side of his neck. She took a moment to revel in the salt of his skin, the clean scent clinging to him. Then she pulled the collar of his shirt aside and nipped at the fleshy pad of muscle where his neck met his shoulder. He groaned, and her core throbbed in eager anticipation. "Take me to bed, Sebastian."

Chapter Four

Sebastian let out a low, agonized groan against her throat. His teeth scraped her shoulder, his nose skimming the side of her neck. Shivers ran the length of Christina's spine as he tightened his arms around her and picked her straight up. Gaze locked on hers and full of a heat that stoked the blaze in her belly, he strode to her bedroom, located at the back of the house. Once inside, he came to a stop at the foot of the bed and set her down, letting her body slide along his.

Christina's heart hammered in her throat, a yearning, terrified pulse. She didn't know what to expect from him or this, so she waited, lost in his hypnotic blue eyes. The hunger and desire in them made her tremble. In anticipation. In need.

Finally, he lifted a hand, stroking her skin with the tips of his fingers. First her cheek, then the shell of her ear, the curve of her shoulder, and around the edge of her left breast. With every small, tender touch, her reservations flew the coop and goose bumps popped up along her skin. Sensation flooded to every cell. God, she hadn't anticipated tenderness. She'd expected sexual prowess. Hot, hard, and fast. Heaven help her, he had her melting to his whim.

When he swiped the pad of his thumb across her tightened nipple, her eyes closed and she dropped her head back. She couldn't deny it. She was his to do with as he saw fit. Tomorrow, the regret would no doubt hit her. When their relationship changed irrevocably. When he walked away. Now she needed him, needed his touch like she needed to draw her next breath.

While his right hand moved to the tie of her robe, working to undo the knot, his soft lips skimmed the exposed column of her throat. His hot tongue occasionally flicked out to singe her skin. He finally pulled off the sash, letting it drop to the floor, and slid his hand inside. "God, what you do to me."

The first touch of his warm palm curling around her breast wrenched a gasp from her. Heated shivers chased each other over the surface of her skin. She reached out blindly, fisting handfuls of his shirt in a desperate attempt to stay upright. "Sebastian…"

His thumb flicked her tightened, aching nipple again. Christina couldn't stop the moan that left her. He'd barely touched her and already she was crumbling. Her fantasies had nothing on the real thing. His hands were smooth and warm, but the tips of his fingers held those wonderful calluses, from years of plucking the strings of his guitar. They added a roughness, a contrast of sensation, that made her shiver. In her fantasies of course, he was always tender and giving, but she hadn't expected him to be that way in reality. She'd always expected he'd be like most of the men in her life, taking his own need. So it still managed to surprise her when he moved slowly, as if he were every bit as awed by her as she was by him. The knowledge melted her every last resolve. Whatever tomorrow brought, she'd deal with it then.

"I want to touch you everywhere, take my time kissing every inch of your skin. I've thought about this moment so many times over the years, when I'd finally have you in my arms. Shit, sweetheart, I'm not sure I have it in me right now to be soft and slow. I need you too much."

The urgency in his tone made her open her eyes. Those blue eyes blazed at her, full of the same hunger pounding through her. He meant what he said, and it amazed her to see the reflection in his eyes. She'd never expected that he'd ever want *her*.

As if in some form of confirmation, his arms tightened around her, pulling her flush against him. His hands slid down her sides to her bottom, anchoring her to him. It didn't escape her notice that he was trembling right along with her.

"I need you, Tina." He leaned his forehead against hers, whispering into the space between them, for that moment so vulnerable and open she could only stare in return.

Had he just laid himself at her feet? The hunger in his eyes made her feel so damned powerful. To know she could do to him what he did to her... she hadn't expected it and the knowledge was intoxicating.

"Tonight I'm yours, Baz." She leaned forward and nipped at his bottom lip, whispering against his mouth in turn. "Fuck me."

"Shit…" He let out another agonized groan and pulled her robe open, exposing her shoulder. His teeth closed over the muscle, scraping lightly. "You're going to make me come right here if you keep talking like that."

She slid her hands up his chest, delighting in the contour of the muscle before finding the first of the buttons on his shirt. Teasing him was a cruel form of torture, but his reactions were addicting. She wanted to revel in them.

She turned her mouth to his ear and whispered the words again. "Fuck me."

His head came up, eyes burning. One corner of his mouth hitched. "You have a dirty mouth."

She stepped back, her hands trembling as she shed her robe. Oh, she'd been naked in front of a man plenty of times, but never with *him*, and it was a damn nerve-wracking moment. Every limb had to be shaking, and her heart caught in her throat as she held her breath, waiting for his reaction. Sebastian was like discovering a whole new world, one where she'd always assumed she'd never fit in. Out of all the men she'd dated, his opinion mattered.

Sebastian's smile melted as his gaze slid over her, taking her in. Hunger flared in his eyes. "My God. You are so damn beautiful."

The awe in his voice filled her with such a sense of feminine power she was sure her chest puffed out. She'd always been the geeky girl. The smart girl. Oh, she worked out to keep in shape, but she spent ninety percent of her time at the office, in business suits. With him looking at her that way, she actually *felt* beautiful, feminine. Sebastian was the first man who made her feel as if he truly saw her and that was a heady, powerful discovery.

He met her gaze again and the tension between them snapped. They reached for each other at the same moment. His arms closed around her, pulling her tight against him, and his mouth settled over hers, hard and hungry. He devoured her, his warm hands sliding to her hips. She attempted the buttons on his shirt with trembling fingers, and Sebastian toed off his shoes, walking her backward.

Her knees hit the bed, and he pressed her back and crawled over her, settling between her thighs. His lean body pressing her into the firm mattress was a luscious sensation she was sure once she'd never get to experience. He covered her mouth with his, kissing her long and languid this time, his tongue stroking hers, and she abandoned the buttons on his shirt and moved lower. When his belt buckle refused to budge, his hand joined hers and between the two of them, they worked to undo his fly. He unlatched his belt, and her trembling fingers undid the button and slid down the zipper.

Finally freed, his cock settled against her stomach. A heady shiver of anticipation moved through her. She caressed her hands down his back, slipped them into his pants, and cupped his ass. She arched tightly against him. Her clit pulsed. She needed this. His cock, hot and hard inside of her, pushing into her, the luscious rush of orgasm, but mostly…she needed the connection to *him*. Right or wrong, whatever happened when the night ended, she needed this time with him.

"Condom." Sebastian nipped at her bottom lip, his mouth curling against hers. "And don't tell me you don't have any. You were always overprepared for everything. If I know you, you've got some stashed away somewhere."

She leaned to her right, reached into the top drawer, and pulled out a foil packet. He was right. Since Craig four years ago, she didn't do commitment. She and Sebastian were a lot alike in that respect. It was a lonely way to live, but it kept men in a safe little box. Not that she brought many home these days. The thrill it used to give her had lost its appeal. She always made sure to keep condoms on hand, though, just in case.

Sebastian pushed upright and kneeled between her thighs. Her gaze was glued to his cock as his deft fingers rolled the condom down his length. She pressed her fingers to her mouth but couldn't contain her giggle. She'd been right. Sebastian's cock wasn't small by any stretch of the imagination. The tip stretched clear to his belly button. He was long and deliciously thick, and her mouth watered just looking at him.

His gaze jerked up. His eyes narrowed, but one corner of his mouth quirked upward. "Never laugh at a man with his cock in his hand, Tina."

His comment and his clear unease had the tension loosening between them. Pink rose in his cheeks, transforming Sebastian from the unobtainable playboy back to the man she'd grown up with. The boy who'd taken great pride in taunting her in primary school. Who'd broken Bobby Stalwart's nose sophomore year in high school because he'd made a derogatory comment about her. Who spent every Thanksgiving and Christmas at her parents' house. The knowledge eased the nervous tangles in her stomach.

"I'm sorry. It's childish, really. I've always wondered how big you were. When you kissed me the other day, you had an erection. I ached to touch you, to find out." Brave now with the ease between them, she rose to kneel in front of him. Gaze locked on his, she straddled his thighs and reached between their bodies, dragging her fingertips lightly up the length of his cock. "I'm pleased to see I was right. You are most definitely not a small boy."

His eyes slid to half-mast. He caressed her thighs and the curve of her hips before closing his hands around her ass. Using the purchase, he pulled her farther up his lap, until the length of him nestled against the folds of her body. He nipped at her bottom lip, murmuring against her mouth. "Thought about my cock, have you?"

Those words from his mouth, the teasing taunt in his tone, had a hot little shiver running through her. She'd long wondered how it would be between them, if the teasing would make its way into the bedroom, too. She was glad to see it did.

She wound her arms around his neck and rubbed her breasts across his chest, delighting in the luscious friction of her nipples against the smattering of dark hair covering his pecs. Then she rose up, sinking down enough to allow the head to slip inside. "A few times."

He groaned, his eyes fluttering closed, and froze. His hands closed almost painfully tight around her ass cheeks. His jaw clenched and a tremor rolled through him. "Shit…You're fucking unmanning me, Tina. I haven't had a hair trigger since I was like nineteen."

She rolled her hips again, and he slipped deeper inside her. His thick cock rubbed sensitive, swollen tissues, setting fire to every nerve ending along the way. She longed to close her eyes and immerse herself in the luscious delight, but his reactions captured her attention. A mix of torment and pleasure rolled across his features. Over the years, she'd had her fair share of lovers, but his reactions were the ultimate turn-on. She wanted to give him the same pleasure he gave her. She had every intention of keeping this at one night. Tomorrow, she would end the insanity between them. Sebastian would never be what she truly wanted. But for this one night, she'd let herself enjoy him, and she wanted to make sure he never forgot their time together.

He growled, low and frustrated and aroused, and opened his eyes. Two seconds later, he flipped her onto her back and flicked his hips against hers, shoving hard into her. Her headboard knocked the wall with the force of his thrust.

Christina gasped with the impact. One thrust and he'd struck the match. Her thighs trembled and her inner muscles tightened. Pleasure rolled through her.

"Sebastian…" Jesus, he felt good. His cock filled every inch of her insides, rubbing all the right places and every nerve ending was like a live wire, lit up and throbbing.

He brushed his mouth over hers, kissing his way across

her jaw. His hot tongue stroked up her neck to the sensitive spot behind her ear. "How many times have you touched yourself while thinking of my cock, hmm?"

He whispered the words and flicked his hips again, shoving into her. Her headboard knocked the wall again. His pelvis rubbed her swollen clit. Tiny tremors skittered across the surface of her skin. Her response caught in her throat, a strangled moan her only coherent reply. Instead, she opted to show him and curled her fingers around his ass, arching against him.

He began a slow, torturous rhythm then, stroking all the way in and all the way out. All the while his mouth traveled her neck, her shoulder, her ear. His warm breath whispered over her skin, his breathing harsh and erratic. She relished every sound, every twitch of muscle. Her body tuned to his, and his every reaction fueled the need burning her up from the inside out. Until she couldn't think, couldn't even remember if she breathed. Completely at his whim, she could only react, let him take her world and spin it beyond her wildest imagination.

"Did you make yourself come while thinking of me? Christ, I think I spent most of high school with my cock in my hand, fantasizing about you. Your sweet mouth, your tight little ass…" He groaned, his body shaking now along with hers. His teeth clamped down on the sensitive spot where her neck met her shoulder. He reached down and hooked her knee, pulled her leg over his hip and increased his tempo, thrusting deeper, harder. "Tell me, Tina. Have you?"

She drew a shuddering breath and attempted to find her brain, to make her tongue work.

"Yes. *Ohhhh, God.* Yes." Another wave of pleasure pulsed through her, and she dragged her fingernails down his back, her toes curling.

Sebastian cursed under his breath. His hips jerked. His breathing hitched, and he paused on an out stroke. His body shook in earnest now, his breath taking on an erratic huff, all of it telling her he'd arrived at the same place she had—lost and overwhelmed.

"You're my favorite fantasy, Baz. That morning you answered the door in your underwear?" She wrapped her arms around him and turned her head, kissing his shoulder, his neck, scraping her teeth over his stubbled jaw. He had her riding that fine sweet edge, on the verge of rupturing, but when she went, she planned to take him with her. "I had an incredible orgasm before getting out of bed, thinking about you, about this."

His head shot up, eyes dark and hungry. Then he bent his head and took her mouth, his tongue thrusting inside. He pushed into her hard, over and over. His lips bruised hers, demanding and coaxing a response. Her body bowed off the bed with each stroke, rising to meet him until, with one last flick of his hips, the tension ruptured. His cock hit the exact right spot inside, and pleasure exploded through her, leaving her trembling and gasping.

Sebastian's body tensed over her and began to shake as his orgasm claimed him. "Fuck. Tina…"

When the trembling stopped, he dropped his forehead

into the crook of her shoulder. They lay that way, for how long she couldn't be certain, holding each other, their harsh breathing the only sound in the room, both trying to catch their breath.

When their breathing finally returned to normal, he rolled off her and collapsed onto the bed beside her. They lay in silence, side by side. She didn't know what to say to him. Their lovemaking amazed her. Never had she imagined it would be that good with him. That he'd far exceeded her expectations had her grinning in spite of herself.

Beside her, Sebastian chuckled, low and still breathless. "Jesus. I always knew it would be intense with you."

Grateful that nothing had changed, she took his playful words and ran with them. Let them fuel her need. He made her feel beautiful, wanted, and for this one night, she intended to take as much as he'd give her.

She rolled onto her side and tucked her hand beneath her pillow, arching a brow at him. "Think you can handle me, cowboy?"

He laughed again and took a moment to take off the condom, wrapped it in a tissue from the box on her nightstand, and tossed it in the small trashcan beside her bed. Then he lay back again and looked over at her. Wickedness glinted in his eyes as he took her hand, slid it down his stomach, and curled her fingers around his length. He was still hard as granite.

He arched a brow, accepting her challenge and tossing it back at her. "I think the question is, sweetheart, whether or not *you* can handle *me*."

She couldn't help the laugh that escaped her. His orgasm hadn't even taken the edge off his erection. She'd heard about guys like him, who could quite literally go all night. She'd never met one, had always figured they were nothing more than guys bragging.

She pushed upright, sliding over the top of him, hands braced on his chest, and straddled his hips. The now slippery folds of her body settled over his length. "What are you, the Energizer Bunny?"

"I've spent years fantasizing about you and here you are, straddling my cock. I've got a lot of time to make up for." His hot hands skimmed her thighs, his touch so light he left goose bumps. Her skin, super-sensitive now postorgasm, came alive all over again. His gaze scorched hers. "Grab another condom, sweetheart. I'm not done with you yet."

She did as he bade, pulling another foil packet from the nightstand and rolling it down his impressive length, then sank onto him with greedy abandon. She shouldn't have allowed the intimacy between them, should not have crossed this line, but his sweet words by the door had done her in. Something was definitely different about him tonight. But did he mean what he'd said? That he actually cared for her? Or was that the needy playboy talking, who just wanted a distraction, like he had the other morning in his kitchen?

The trouble was, she didn't know, which was why she would allow herself to enjoy this night with him, but tomorrow it had to end. All too soon her alarm would go off and the dawn would bring an ugly dose of reality. Sebastian would kiss her sweetly, make his excuses, and leave, if he stayed at all. Then the awkwardness would begin. He'd go back to treating her like Caden's sister, and she'd have to pretend his casual attitude didn't hurt like hell. Would have to go back to watching him with other women and pretend it wasn't a knife in her heart. He'd no doubt avoid her like the plague. For every Christmas or Thanksgiving that they got together with family, the way they'd done since they were kids, the tension created would forever be an awkward wall between them. Their dark little secret. She'd fucked Caden's best friend.

For tonight, though, he was hers, and she'd get to fulfill a long-standing fantasy. She'd deal with the consequences when the alarm went off in the morning.

* * *

"Sebastian. Sebastian, wake up."

Whether she was real or part of the delicious dream he was having, Sebastian allowed Christina's soft voice to coax his eyes open. She sat on the side of the bed. Nope, not a dream. In fact, she must have showered, for she was fully dressed, wearing another of her mind-blowing pencil skirts. With her white shirt left open and her hair tied back in bun, he could admire her slender throat and the nape of her neck. Beautiful. Her stiff posture and the nervous edge in her gaze, though, told him something was wrong. She looked like she was prepared to flee at a moment's notice.

"You're actually here. I thought, perhaps, you were a dream." He smiled, reaching for the hand resting in her lap.

"You're entirely too dressed for this early in the morning. Come back to bed."

Instead of allowing him to pull her to him, she drew her hand out of reach. Something flitted through her gaze, there and gone before he'd fully caught it, but it looked a lot like alarm. The same emotion sank inside of him, tightening his stomach. Okay, something was definitely off.

"Good morning, Sebastian. I'm sorry to run, but I have an eight o'clock meeting. I took the liberty of calling your assistant. She says your first meeting isn't until ten." She turned to the nightstand and lifted a ceramic mug in his direction. The pleasant smile she flashed wobbled. "I've made coffee. Strong and black, the way you like it. These are an extra set of keys. If you could lock the door when you leave, I'd appreciate it. You can leave the keys with Caden or drop them by my office. My assistant will make sure I get them."

Oh, he got the message, loud and clear. The night was over and she'd relegated him to "morning after" mode. It was a clear but subtle "the night is over. Please see yourself out." Whatever good mood he'd woken with evaporated. In its place, a foreign emotion he didn't want to look too closely at seized his chest. It felt an awful lot like disappointment.

He sat up and moved around her, scooting to the end of the bed. A glance at the clock on the nightstand told him it was a little after seven thirty. He'd have time to go home and shower before his day began, though last night, he'd envisioned this morning going slightly different. He shouldn't have come over. His intention had been to drink himself into a stupor so he wouldn't be able to think, to ponder his father's death. Like it or not, the hurt had settled in, and he hadn't a damn clue how to reconcile it.

He'd never been more alone in his life and Christina had been a lure he should've resisted but hadn't been able to. He had so many regrets, so many things he should've told his father while he was still alive and damn the consequences. He hated the thought of Christina being one of them. The liquor had done what it always did, loosened his inhibitions, and he'd decided she wouldn't be one of his regrets. Maybe he wouldn't be able to touch her after he said what he needed to, but he'd intended to right things between them.

Except once again, she'd responded. When he touched her, she shuddered. When he kissed her, her mouth softened beneath his. The heat in her eyes and that damn soft way she had about her had done him in. He'd needed her.

He'd hoped at the very least to spend the morning relishing the intimacy with her. Maybe they'd have breakfast together and talk. Maybe he'd make love to her one more time before he had to let her go.

"I'm well aware of what this is and what it isn't, but 'get dressed and get out' is a little cold even for you." He rose from the bed and gathered his clothing off the floor where he'd flung it the night before.

She didn't move but remained where she sat, back ramrod straight. Her awareness of him prickled in the air around him. Despite her cool exterior, her eyes followed his every move, and she clenched her hands in her lap so tightly her knuckles had turned white. "It was a one-night stand, Sebastian, and it's over. Let's not drag this out."

As he pulled his shorts on, he jerked his gaze to hers. Anger rose like a tide within him. He'd never be able to forget the experience. She'd left her mark on him, in more ways than one. Judging by the soreness, his back contained proof positive of the heat generated between them. It had to be ironic, really. Wasn't this usually the man's job the next morning?

He shot her a glance as he stepped into his pants. "As long as we've known each other, I hoped you might treat me with a little more warmth and respect. But whatever. You do what you need to do to separate yourself from this."

She blinked. "Have I offended you? I would think you'd be grateful I was leaving quietly."

Her words sank hard and cold in his chest. He'd always known that was what she thought of him, because he'd done it on purpose, but to see it in her eyes, hear the disappointment in her quiet voice, was too much. This time, he couldn't leave it that way.

Clothing disregarded for the moment, he moved back to the bed and bent over her, hands braced on her thighs, so he had her undivided attention. "You have a lot of wrong ideas about me, sweetheart. I've always let you believe what you wanted, because you're my best friend's sister and it created a safe barrier between us. Since we've blown that barrier to kingdom come, I'm going to set you straight. I've never in my life treated a woman like she was another warm body. It's not my style. I'm actually fond of the morning after. Mine usually end with breakfast. I make no promises, so I don't ever *need* to talk my way out of anything. So, if you need some space to separate yourself from this, I can deal with that, but have the balls to be straight with me."

He straightened and finished getting dressed, pulling on and buttoning his shirt, finding his socks and his shoes. Silence rose over the room, the air prickling with tension. Christina's gaze followed his every move, but he forced himself to focus on his task and refused to look at her. After all, she did him a favor by putting distance between them and neatly severing whatever tie they'd formed last night.

Making love to a woman was supposed to create intimacy. Making love to the one woman he actually cared about had done nothing but widen the rift between them. This damn night should never have happened.

Christina rose from the bed, hands fisted at her sides, and pinned him with a hard stare. He didn't miss the way her lower lip trembled, but stubborn woman that she was, she stuck her chin in the air.

"Fine. You really want to know what I'm thinking? I had the luxury of waking up next to you this morning. I lay there for a few minutes, watching you sleep." She let out a harsh laugh. "Pathetic, right? So, you'll have to forgive me for being a bit cold, but I've been here before, and I have no desire to watch you fumble for an excuse about how this can't happen again. I already know that. So consider me saving you the trouble."

She didn't give him a chance to respond but strode past him and out the bedroom door. The sound of her heels *click-clacking* across the hardwood floors filled the unbearable silence that rose over the house, followed by the front door snapping shut. Thirty seconds later, an engine roared to life in her garage. He made his way to the window and nudged the pale blue curtain aside in time to catch the tail of her silver BMW speeding away from the house.

He also noted the limo. Outside, sitting along the curb, his driver waited, leaning back against the car, arms folded. The sight nudged a sore spot inside, yet filled him with awe. Not only had she called his driver for him, but she'd also woken him, knowing his daily schedule, and had even made him coffee exactly the way he liked it. Once again, she had no idea how much she tended to act like his wife, like they shared something more than they did. The knowledge taunted him. He'd already crossed the line with her, had already laid his heart out on a flippin' platter. If ever there was a woman worth taking a risk on, it was her. So what was to stop him from doing exactly that?

The thoughts circled in his mind as he shoved his feet into his shoes and made his way toward the front door. After closing up the house, he met his driver at the curb. Miles wasn't much older than him. He was a tall man. In his black uniform and sunglasses, the man reminded him of a CIA operative, but he did his job with excellence. Best driver he'd had in years.

Miles smiled politely as he pulled open the passenger door. "Where to, sir?"

Sebastian returned a tired smile. "Home, please. I'll need a shower and a quick change; then I'll be heading into the office."

"Yes, sir."

Sebastian climbed inside and settled back against the leather seats. As the limo pulled away from the curb, he sighed and stared out the window. As the houses and trees blurred past, one thought stood out above the rest. Christina had clearly expected him to make his excuses and leave. Which one meant thing: She didn't trust him. He ought to be glad for it, but he couldn't drum up the emotion for the life of him. The knowledge was a tumor growing in his gut. He wanted, more than anything, to prove to her he wasn't like the other jerks in her life. Hell, to prove to her he wasn't the jerk he'd always shown her. He wanted to prove to himself as well that he wasn't his father.

Which meant things had to change.

By the time the limo pulled into the parking garage of his building, the decision had made itself. He had to earn Christina's trust or die trying.

Chapter Five

Christina stared down at the white bakery box on her desk. Over the last two weeks, she'd received a bevy of things like it. Every day since she'd last seen Sebastian, she'd arrived at her work to find a hot cup of Starbucks coffee on her desk. A vanilla latte with no whipped cream and fat-free milk. The first had come with a handwritten note:

A peace offering. To get you through the morning.
~Sebastian

When the fifth arrived, she'd finally asked Paula. She said he stopped in every morning. How the hell he managed to beat her to work, she didn't know, but he hadn't stopped there, either. Every day lunch had been delivered via a messenger. Again, the first came with another handwritten note:

I know you have a tendency to skip lunch in favor of work. You're not doing anybody any good if you don't stop to eat.
~Sebastian

The trouble was, he was right. She *did* have a tendency to skip lunch. Especially now with the software release coming in two weeks. This was always the busiest time, to make sure nothing went wrong on release day.

Today's surprise was a box of cookies. Peanut butter cookies to be exact. This one, though, hadn't come with a note. She didn't have to ask to know these were likely from Sebastian as well. Mrs. Humphreys, her parents' housekeeper when she and Caden were kids, always made sure there was a fresh, warm batch when they got home from school every day. Nine times out of ten, Sebastian would come home with them. She had so many memories of the three of them, sitting in the kitchen, chomping down cookies and swallowing them with glasses of milk. Ever since, peanut butter cookies had always reminded her of home.

She released a heavy sigh, leaned back in her chair, and turned her gaze to the white textured ceiling. What she'd wanted was time. She was struggling with the aftermath of their night together. With any other man, she had no problem walking away. Sebastian was just different. They couldn't go back from this. Neither could she forget. Truth be told, she wasn't certain she wanted to, or even could, think of him as just a friend now. So she'd put her head down and focused on work.

And now this. Clearly he had a reason for doing it, but what? Sebastian had never showered her with quite so much before. Oh, he took her out for lunch on her birthday every year. Christmas they always exchanged gifts. But up until the day his father died, he'd always been rather…indifferent toward her. While the gifts were sweet, she still hadn't a clue which side of him was real.

How was she supposed to react to this after the way things had ended between them? Call and thank him and pretend nothing had changed? She wasn't sure she could pull it off anymore.

Before she could decide, her phone buzzed from its position on the corner of her desk. Sebastian's number flashed on the screen. Apparently, she couldn't avoid him either.

She sat forward, snatched up her phone, and punched the ACCEPT button. "Sebastian, what is all this?"

"So you got them."

She closed her eyes. It was the first time in two weeks that they'd really spoken. Oh, he'd called, and she'd texted to thank him for the coffee and the lunches, but the sound of his voice on a machine had nothing on him live. His rich, smooth rumble slid along the phone line like a hot caress, sending a shower of sparks over the surface of her skin.

She sighed. This. This was why she'd been avoiding him. What she needed was time to find her center again, to find some kind of equilibrium where he was concerned, but how the hell could she do that when just the sound of his voice weakened her defenses?

"I got the cookies. Thank you. Peanut butter is my favorite." She swallowed a miserable groan. Of course he knew that.

"Mrs. Humphreys's cookies. You mentioned her that morning. You were babbling at me while you made breakfast. I remember those peanut butter cookies she used to make. You know I don't cook, so these are from that bakery you love in Pike Place Market."

She squeezed her eyes closed and drew a deep breath. Damn it all to hell. He had to go and say that. "It's very sweet, Baz, but it doesn't change anything."

A soft creak sounded over the line, the sound a chair makes when it's tipped backward, and her head filled with visions of him in his office. "Do you know in all the years we've known each other, you've never really stopped speaking to me? Oh, you tried once, in fifth grade, because I was an ass and I deserved it. But it was only for a couple of days."

Heart hammering, she opened her eyes, staring for a moment at her office door some ten feet beyond her desk. "I'm surprised you remember that."

"I remember everything, Tina." He spoke the words with the same low, tender tone. "Since then, you've always gotten in my face and yelled at me. I can't count on all ten fingers and toes the numbers of times I was sick and you barged into my condo and insisted on taking care of me. But since that night we spent together, you've been avoiding me and it tells me something. Loud and clear."

Don't ask. Cut the call short and don't ask. At least, that's what the logical side of her brain told her.

The side of her that desperately wanted to get back to some semblance of normal, however, wouldn't let her *not* ask. Before they'd slept together, she wouldn't have hesitated to call and thank him. Or spend a few minutes chatting. "Told you what?"

"That you don't trust me. Which is what all this is."

"An attempt to re-earn my trust?" God, was it even possible?

"As a start. To show you that I meant it when I said I see you."

Christina's heart kicked up its pace, thundering through her chest. Not for the first time this morning, his words threatened to melt her every defense.

The office door opened and her assistant, Paula, poked her head inside. "I'm sorry to interrupt, Miss McKenzie, but your eleven o'clock is here."

Grateful for the interruption, she sat forward, held the phone away from her mouth, and smiled at Paula.

"Thank you, Paula. Give me five minutes?" When Paula nodded and closed the door, she turned back to the phone. "Baz, I'm afraid I have to go. I have a meeting with the head of IT. The new software launches in two weeks, and it's a madhouse around here."

"Always is before a launch." His voice held a smile, a warmth that slid along her nerve endings. "Don't stress. You have very good attention to detail. Things will go off without a hitch, the way they always do."

"I sure hope so." She hesitated, heart hammering in her ears. To tell him this was laying her cards on the table again, but even a friend would say thank you. Right? "Thank you for the cookies. It was a sweet gesture."

"You're welcome. I'll see you at the auction, Tina."

The hint of anticipation in his voice had the same emotion sliding along her nerve endings.

"See you at the auction." She hung up her phone and laid

it on her desk before dropping back in her chair. The auction. Where she could no longer hide from him, but would, instead, be face-to-face with him. God help her.

* * *

Masculine laughter rang through the near empty ballroom, sending Christina's pulse skittering. Standing beside the bar on the far right of the square room, the light and fluffy conversation she'd been having with the women seated beside her went forgotten. They'd been discussing the bachelors, biding their time until the auction started in a half hour.

Now the hairs on the back of her neck prickled. Warmth flooded her insides, and whatever she'd been about to say flew right out of her head as her senses honed in on Sebastian. Oh, she didn't have to look to know the laughter was his. She'd been hearing that laugh for twenty years.

There was still a lot of setup to be done, to make sure the evening went without a hitch, but the thought of seeing him again had her on edge since she'd arrived two hours ago. Her whole body trembled, waiting for the moment when he'd show up.

Music played over the loudspeakers in the room, soft and low, but did nothing to soothe her nerves. She picked up her half-empty champagne flute off the bar and tipped its contents into her mouth.

She touched the shoulder of the brunette to her right. "Excuse me, ladies."

Then she sent up a silent prayer, straightened her shoulders, and forced herself to turn around. The two women beside her, lonely housewives in their forties whose husbands traveled for work, turned to flirt with the young bartender.

Their conversation faded to a muted hum behind her as Christina's gaze found Sebastian across the room. He and Caden stood off to the left of the entryway. The two appeared to be having a relaxed conversation.

He looked spectacular, as usual. His black Armani tux fit him to perfection, showcasing his broad shoulders and long legs. Soaking shamelessly in the sight of him, the memory of waking beside him hit her full force. After their intimate conversation at work two weeks ago, the memory refused to leave her. Waking with him pressed against her back, like two nesting spoons, his arm flung over her waist, fingers curled around her left breast like it belonged there.

Closing her eyes to gather herself, the soft stir of his warm breath against the nape of her neck rushed back at her, so vivid and so real, the same shivers ran the length of her spine all over again.

For the first time since she'd started these fund-raisers three years ago, she didn't look forward to the evening. Seeing him was throwing her for a loop. Something was definitely different about him. She couldn't ignore that. But neither was she ready to see him.

God, if only Maddie and Hannah were here. They'd talk her down from the rafters. Since making full partner at their father's law office in San Diego a few years back, Caden hadn't come home as much. She'd missed him. He'd moved home again officially after he and Hannah got together, and

Christina spent as much time with the two of them as he'd allow.

She and Maddie had gotten together to plan Hannah's bachelorette party. The three of them had so much fun it became a weekly tradition, getting together for coffee, lunch, or an afternoon movie. Always having been one of the smart girls, she'd spent most of her childhood with her head in books. Reading, absorbing and learning as much as she could had always been her addiction. Her idea of fun were the experiments in chemistry class. Which meant she'd never had gaggles of friends. Caden had always been her confidant. It was good to have girlfriends.

Maddie had promised to come but as of yet hadn't arrived. Caden stood alone with Sebastian, though. Had Hannah stayed home? Had the morning sickness become too much?

"He looks good in a tux. It suits him."

At Hannah's soft, familiar voice, Christina glanced beside her. She and Maddie stood to the right of the bar, both of them wearing knowing smiles. Despite her embarrassment at having been caught ogling, relief flooded her, relaxing the knot in her stomach. Now she wouldn't have to face tonight alone.

"Oh, I'm so glad you made it." Unable to hide her enthusiasm, she stepped forward, enveloping each of them in a hug, then stood back, eyeing Hannah. Her gorgeous dress flowed over her curves. She looked beautiful and feminine, and she glowed, but at six months pregnant, she looked uncomfortable. She also looked a little green around the gills. Christina flashed a worried frown. "How are you feeling? I take it the morning sickness isn't getting any better?"

"I'm afraid not. As long as I eat regularly, it's not as bad, so I made sure I had something before we left the house." Hannah frowned, lips pursed, and stroked a hand over her rounded belly. "I swear by the time this baby's born, I'm going to be as fat as a house. I've already lost sight of my feet."

Christina rubbed her arm. "Oh, nonsense. You're beautiful. I'm jealous. You have that glow."

Hannah smiled, her golden brown eyes alight, as if she'd caught wind of a secret.

"Funny. You have the same glow this evening." She nodded in the direction of the men across the ballroom. "Sebastian got here the same time we did. He caught us on the way in. You should go over and say hello."

Christina turned to eye Sebastian again and sighed. Any other time, she wouldn't have hesitated to greet him as he arrived for the auction. She'd always played the part of the gracious hostess, and she was always grateful for his participation. Now, regret and longing warred for supremacy in her stomach. So much had changed between them.

Hannah drew her brows together, studying her. "Something happened between the two of you."

At Hannah's astute observation, Christina straightened her shoulders and turned back to the girls. Normally she shared everything with them, but she hadn't shared this. She hadn't wanted it to get back to Caden. Hadn't wanted to face the aftermath at all. "And I'm not ready to face him again yet."

Maddie nodded at something beyond her. "Then you better brace yourself, sweetie. He's heading in our direction."

Christina swiveled, following Maddie's gaze. Her stomach tightened. Maddie was right. Where Caden walked at a casual pace, Sebastian stalked several steps ahead, his stride long and purposeful, his gaze set on her, piercing and determined.

"Oh God." Christina set her shoulders, trying to summon her courage, to prepare herself for the contact. "What on earth do I say to him?"

Making love to him hadn't at all been a casual romp in the hay, as she'd expected, the way she'd experienced with most of the men she'd been with over the years. Sebastian was familiar. His touch on her body might have been a new sensation, but the act itself had seemed oddly like déjà vu. Like they'd made love a thousand times. He made her long to get lost in the blue sea of his eyes, lost in his warm touch. Waking in his arms had thrown her for a loop, if only because it had felt so damn right. His body beside her in bed had felt as natural as taking a breath.

She'd hoped the last month would have given her the time she needed, but all the gifts he'd sent had left her feeling as if she stood on a fault line. They hadn't talked again since that conversation two weeks ago. Oh, she'd texted to thank him but hadn't called him back. She'd apologized, giving him the excuse that she was busy. It wasn't even an excuse, really. It was the truth. Last month's software release had gone off without a hitch. Sales were better than expected, but profits were still down. They needed to brainstorm, come up with new marketing initiatives or they'd never compete in this market.

Suddenly there he was, and she wasn't any more ready for this moment. How in the world did she pretend she didn't know every inch of his body intimately?

Maddie stepped up to her side and laid a reassuring hand on her back. "Relax, sweetie. Just be your natural charming self."

As the men came close, Caden stopped behind Hannah, slipped his arms around her, and settled his hands on her stomach. He bent his head, kissing her shoulder, and whispered something in her ear. Watching the two of them always filled her with conflicting sensations. Caden had had a hard time with women. They'd used him. Before Hannah, his last girlfriend had attempted to blackmail him. To see him happy filled her chest to near bursting. It relaxed a knot somewhere inside. She didn't have to worry about him anymore. Hannah would take care of him now.

Seeing them together, though, had envy kicking her hard in the stomach. Would she ever have that for herself? She'd long ago stopped believing in love. She didn't know if love was possible for her. Most men either saw her father's billions or the computer geek who worked too much. Caden's happiness had drummed up the schoolgirlish desire all over again. She'd been lonely for too long.

Sebastian stepped into her line of sight, snapping her perusal of the happy couple shut and forcing her gaze to him. Christina attempted a smile, but before her polite greeting could even leave her tongue, he folded his arms, pinning her with an intense, focused stare that had her breath catching in her throat. "Don't think I didn't notice the way you've been avoiding me these last two weeks. Now that I've got your undivided attention, there are a few things I'd like to say to you."

Hannah smiled and reached for Caden's hand. "We'll give you two some privacy. I could use a drink, anyway."

Sebastian lifted a hand in Hannah's direction but didn't take his eyes off Christina. "No, it's okay. I'd like witnesses so she can't misconstrue this later."

Christina took a step back, but Sebastian hooked an arm around her waist, stopping her retreat. He arched a brow. The glint in his eye challenged her to deny him. When she couldn't—because he held her too tightly—he hooked both arms around her, his warm hands settling on the bare skin of her back where her dress cut low.

"For the record, you need to know I do these shindigs for you and you alone. I'm here because this is your baby, and I want you to succeed. I also happen to think breast cancer research is a good cause. But make no mistake. I have never and will never go home with any of these women. I go on my requisite date, we have a little fun, I flirt because it makes them feel good, but I go home very much alone."

Her cheeks heated a thousand degrees. Of all the things for him to say in front of Caden. She pushed against his chest, attempting to free herself from his addicting hold, but to no avail. "Baz, please. This isn't the time or the place for this."

Sebastian's arm tightened around her, holding firm. As

she was five foot ten, he stood only six inches taller. In heels, she nearly matched him in height, and his every breath blew warm against her lips, teasing her with how close he was.

That he was aroused hadn't escaped her notice, either. Sebastian was hard as steel, and holding her against his solid body, every ridge of that erection pressed into her stomach. She couldn't be certain if that was good or bad, that her presence affected him to that degree. The knowledge sent all manner of hot tingles shooting along her nerve endings and had giddy butterflies taking flight in her stomach. It did nothing, however, for the distance she attempted to achieve with him.

His hands stroked her back, his fingers skimming her spine in an idle fashion that drove her to distraction.

"Oh, on the contrary, this is the perfect time. With them here, you'll actually be quiet long enough for me say what I came to say." Amusement glinted in his eyes. One corner of his mouth quirked upward, but his cheeky smile quickly disappeared. "I thought, perhaps, the gifts would help ease things between us. Since clearly I was wrong, then you should also know that whether we spend one night or three years together, you will never be just another notch on my bedpost. There's a reason I've always stayed away from you."

Christina clenched her jaw to keep her mouth from dropping open. The heat in her cheeks deepened, fire and perspiration pricking along her skin.

"I cannot believe you said that in front of everybody." Unable to bear facing him or the others, she jerked her gaze to the right. Now, if only the floor would open up and swallow her whole. Caden now knew in no uncertain terms that she'd slept with Sebastian. Her only saving grace at this point was the emptiness of the ballroom. Luckily for her, the auction didn't start for another half hour, and only a few people had arrived early. Those who had were gathered in groups, either at the bar or by the dance floor.

"Last but not least, when this evening ends, you and I are going to talk. If you disappear in an attempt to put me off again, I *will* hunt you down, and believe me, I know all your hiding spots." Apparently not finished torturing her, Sebastian pressed a tender kiss to her cheek, his voice warm and husky in her ear. "You look beautiful, by the way."

As quickly as he'd grabbed her, he released her, then pivoted and strode off, leaving her to stare after him. For several moments, she could only remember the in and out of breathing as she tried desperately to collect herself. If she moved, she wasn't certain her wobbly knees would hold her up. Everything south of the equator begged her to go after him and drag him into a closet somewhere. Memories of making love to him ran rampant in her mind. The softness of his lips on her skin. Those warm hands gripping her hips.

Sebastian Blake had two things no man she'd dated ever had—stamina and a libido that matched hers. Being a woman with a high libido had been fun once upon a time, until she realized most men couldn't keep up with her. Most of them found their own orgasms, rolled over, and went to sleep. Sebastian made sure she went with him, then rolled *her* over and kept going.

It didn't help—at all—that he'd floored her with his

speech. Once again, he'd shown her that he truly did see her. That he knew her better than she'd always assumed. But the question remained. Was it all an act? Or was this really the first true peek into the heart of the man that he'd ever shown her?

Beside her, Hannah giggled. Christina turned her head to find them all staring at her, every face grinning from ear to ear. Clearly they'd enjoyed the show. Including Caden. The traitor.

Maddie laughed and slung an arm around her shoulders. "Oh, sweetie, I like him. He's a keeper."

Christina shot Maddie a phony glare but couldn't quite hold back a reciprocating grin.

"I'm so glad you all are having fun at my expense." She turned her head and waved a finger in Caden's direction. "And you. Aren't you supposed to stick up for me?"

Caden shook his head.

"You were doing fine all on your own. You stopped needing me to stick up for you a long time ago. Besides, I'm sorry to tell you this, but I'm on his side. I've watched the two of you pine for each other for far too many years. I've been seriously contemplating locking the two of you in a room together. So, I'm afraid, sis, all I have to say is it's about damn time." He slipped an arm around Hannah's back and leaned down to nuzzle her ear. "Now, if you'll excuse me, I believe my wife said she was thirsty. Then I'd like a dance before the auction starts."

* * *

Standing on the small stage at the front of the room two hours later, Christina drew a deep breath as she stared out over the raucous audience. The square room was full to capacity, bodies in every seat lining the front of the stage, and a few stragglers standing around the edges. As usual, it was mostly women, anywhere from their forties to their sixties, all of them dressed in evening gowns and their finest jewels.

The auction was two hours in, and so far, she'd raised a little over four million for breast cancer research. The night had been hugely successful, and every face beamed. They had a blast, as she'd hoped.

Sebastian was the last bachelor to be auctioned off. Her heart hammered from the vicinity of her throat. This was the part of the auction she loathed. Every year, he pulled some stunt on stage to ramp up the crowd. The first year, he'd gone so far as to strip down to his bare chest, much to the delight of the women in attendance. She'd watched it all wondering which woman he'd end up with. Now she couldn't help wondering if he had told her the truth, if his antics were all an act. If he would go home alone.

She didn't know, and this year, she had no desire to watch and find out. Right or wrong, she needed some semblance of a boundary.

She looked down at her notes for something else to focus on other than the sick sensation twisting in her stomach and drew a shaky breath. Then she plastered on the brightest smile she could muster and forced herself to face the audience. "All right, ladies, our last bachelor of the evening is a man I'm sure some of you know, because you personally requested his presence. For those of you new to the auction this year, allow me to introduce Sebastian Blake."

As he stepped up the podium beside her, Sebastian nudged her with an elbow and leaned toward her. "Don't forget what I said. This is for you and only you."

His words came as a bare murmur between them, so quiet she glanced at him to be sure she hadn't imagined them. He didn't look at her but stared out at the crowd, his smile bright and flirtatious. As per his usual class-clown routine, he folded a hand over his stomach and made a gallant bow. When he straightened, he had the nerve to wrap an arm around her shoulders. "How about a round of applause for our gracious hostess as well, hmm? We have her to thank for this evening. This benefit is her baby. Without her, this evening wouldn't be possible."

Smiles lit up each face, a polite applause rolling through the room.

Christina's face heated. Oh, for sure he laid it on thick tonight. She shrugged out of his embrace and waved a good-natured hand at the audience. "Thank you, but it's for a good cause. How many of you or your friends and love ones have fallen to this disease? Our family has had more than its fair share. We, like many of you, want to find a cure."

An older woman in the front row nodded and held up a hand. "Here, here!"

Christina forced a bright smile and winked at the audience. "All right, ladies, now for the good stuff. 'Baz,' as his friends know him, is the CEO of the family-owned and operated Blake Hotels and Resorts. He's been nominated one of Seattle's most eligible bachelors three years in a row. He's thirty-two and plays guitar—and plays well, I might add."

To this a woman in her twenties called out from the back of the room. "Sing us a song!"

Christina's smile faltered. Part of her job was to encourage stuff like this, to encourage the audience to let their hair down and have a little fun. Woman who were relaxed and having fun spent more money without blinking an eye, and this really was a cause their family believed in. Her father made a large donation every year. The hard part was knowing this was where Sebastian's antics usually began. She had no desire to know how he'd top Caden's romantic display last year.

Caden had been one of the bachelors last year. Like Sebastian, he'd participated every year since she'd started running them. Unbeknownst to her, he'd begun seeing Hannah, had made her a promise the auction would have forced him to break, so they'd devised a plan. The idea had been that Hannah would make the bid for him, but at the height of the auction, instead of bidding, she'd quietly left the room. Having realized she'd fallen in love with him, she couldn't bear the thought of someone else winning his bid.

Seeing her leave had devastated Caden. Then and there, he'd taken himself out of the running by admitting to the entire audience that the women he loved was leaving. Then he promised to match every bid and leapt from the stage, following Hannah out into the hallway.

Bids had gone up all over the room. Within five minutes, he had the highest total of the night. A cool three million.

Beside her, Sebastian laughed, drawing her from the memory. He winked at the woman in the back of the room. "Win my bid, and I can probably be coaxed out of a song or two."

Attempting to go with the flow, Christina forced a laugh. "As my brother's best friend, I've heard him sing. He has a swoon-worthy voice, ladies."

Sebastian nudged her, his voice once again a low murmur meant only for her ears. "I wrote a couple of those songs for you, you know."

Those words had her faltering. She clenched her jaw to keep it from dropping open. All the times over the years she'd sat listening to him pluck the strings of his guitar drifted through her mind. He'd played in a band there for a while, hard rock, of course, loud, intense tunes about rebellion. Sitting by himself, he'd often sing straight from the heart. He had a beautiful voice, deep and velvety. The kind that drew you in and made you swoon because the words hit you right in the heart. She'd always wondered who he sang them for. He'd never tell her, but she'd always listened, envious of the girl he clearly sang for.

Had he truly written some for her? Her heart hammered. Surely not. Yet his words the night of his father's funeral came again. *"I see you... I've always seen you."*

All the little gifts he'd been sending this month.

She drew her shoulders back and forced herself to ignore him, smiling again at the audience. "You'll also be pleased to know our Baz is a cat lover. His furry companion is a three-year-old tabby he coaxed in off the street. Which means, despite his antics, he's a great big softie. You're getting the total package, ladies. In addition to an evening with him, you're also getting a weekend of being pampered at his spa resort here in Seattle. All right, shall we start the bidding?"

Cheers rang out around the audience. She stepped back as the auctioneer took her place at the podium and the feeding frenzy began. With every bid that came in, Sebastian took something off, egging on the women. He started with his jacket, dropping it to the floor, much to the delight of the women. Bids went up all over the room.

By the time the bidding ended, he'd lost his bow tie, both gold cuff links, and four of the buttons on his shirt. A woman in the back of the room, the same one who'd demanded a song, ended the bidding with an outrageous bid of two million no one wanted to counter.

Christina congratulated the woman and turned back to the audience, thanking everyone for coming. As the crowd slowly disbursed, Sebastian trotted down the steps to greet the woman who'd won his bid. Whoever she was, she was gorgeous. About Christina's age, a bottle blonde but with a short, voluptuous stature. She had to hand it to him, though. He drew in the biggest bid of the night. This year was the most successful yet. At least he'd managed to keep his shirt on this time.

He was still walking into the audience, and despite his earlier assurance, doubt grabbed her by the heart. When he greeted the woman by wrapping her in a warm, familiar hug, an ugly emotion tangled in Christina's chest. Trying not to look too hard at it, she turned and left the stage. Her part was over. She didn't want to know any more if he meant what he'd said. She had no desire to see whatever happened next.

* * *

Sebastian leaned back against the bar's edge and took a long pull from his beer. It was well past 10:00 p.m. The auction had officially ended an hour ago. The ballroom had emptied to only the fund-raiser crew and a few stragglers. Across the room, Christina stood at the door, bidding farewell to the last of the guests as they exited. She smiled, her face alight, and tipped her head back and laughed, then wrapped the woman across from her in a hug. He couldn't help the smile that tugged at the corners of his mouth. She was a gracious host. Making people feel comfortable was what she did best, and by God she was beautiful doing it.

With the exception of the auction itself, she'd managed to avoid him for most of the night by being "busy." Watching her had twisted his insides in knots. She'd taken his gifts this month the way she did everything—with politeness and sweetness. And while they'd chatted a time or two, he'd distinctly noticed the distance she continued to attempt to put between them.

Her reactions during the auction had gotten to him as well. Twice as she introduced him her voice had faltered, though she smiled through the whole process. When the bidding ended, her smile lacked its usual warm glow. It looked a little too…forced.

He'd never noticed the reaction before, but according to Cade, she reacted that way every year. How the hell had he managed to be so damned blind when it came to her? He'd put walls up, determined to keep her at a safe distance, to keep her in a place where he couldn't ever lose her. Apparently, he'd accomplished it in spades. She didn't seem to believe that everything he did at these shindigs was for her benefit. And who could blame her? He'd spent too many years building the walls between them.

Hopefully after tonight, that would change. Since clearly his subtle tactics weren't working, she was forcing him to take more drastic measures. If he ever hoped to earn her trust, they would need to spend actual time together.

Luckily, Cade had come through for him. One of the young lawyers in his office had agreed to bid on his behalf, in exchange for a week's stay at any of the resorts. Sebastian would pay the bid, of course, and had agreed to fly her anywhere she wanted to go so long as she made certain no one else topped her bid. He hoped Christina would recognize Stacy, that it would set her at ease, but somehow she hadn't.

"Everything's set." Cade appeared at his side. He leaned against the bar and held out a set of keys. "The limo will be waiting outside. Hannah has no problem taking your Mercedes home. The cabin's stocked. Jan promises me she left you enough supplies for two weeks."

Sebastian had a plan. One that would, with any luck, sweep one Christina McKenzie clean off her heels—literally. He hoped that, once alone, where she couldn't run from him or put him off again, she'd agree to spend the weekend with him.

Cade had helped by offering to switch cars and the use of his family's cabin on Lake Washington. He'd also promised not to spill the beans to Christina. With any luck, by the time the weekend ended, she'd forgive him and she'd finally see him. He didn't know what would happen after that. Only that he had to try.

"Here's hoping it won't take that long." Sebastian glanced over at Cade. "Thank you. It means a lot that you helped me with this."

Cade smiled in return, a gleam in his eye that said he understood, in a way only best friends could. "I wouldn't trust her with anybody but you. You're one of the few, save myself and Father, who I know would take a bullet for her."

Sebastian took a pull off his beer. He didn't have to think about his response. Cade was right. "In a heartbeat."

"Exactly why I trust you." Cade hitched a shoulder.

Sebastian gave a slow shake of his head. Doubt rose over him, settling hard and cold in his stomach. "I don't know what the hell I'm doing, man. This might not even work."

"Neither did I, which is why you should trust it." Cade bumped his shoulder, then straightened off the bar and grinned. "Good luck. I'm taking Hannah and getting the hell out of Dodge. If Chris finds out I had a hand in this, she'll have my balls."

Cade strode off, finding Hannah chatting with Christina and Maddie. Sebastian spent the next ten minutes nursing his beer, waiting for the right time. When the last of the guests finally left, he downed the contents of his glass and set it on the countertop along with a tip for the bartender. He pushed away from the bar and headed for Christina. Talking now with another of the directors from the fund-raiser, she darted a glance in his direction; her back stiffened but otherwise she didn't so much as acknowledge him.

The woman she spoke with, mid-fifties with unnaturally blond hair and seeming to wear every piece of jewelry she had, offered him a warm smile. "You provided another showstopper tonight, Sebastian."

He smiled politely in return. "Just doing my part, Grace. Hope it increases profits this year. I hope you'll forgive the intrusion, but I'd like to steal your cohort."

Grace nodded and waved a hand at him. "Oh, we're finished for the night. Steal away. Take her somewhere nice. It's her turn to relax now."

He stifled a laugh. If only she knew.

"You have my solemn promise." He made a crisscross motion over his heart and turned to Christina. "Forgive me."

"Please, Baz, not here." Stubborn woman that she was, Christina hiked her chin a notch and shook her head, refusing even to look at him, then pivoted and walked off.

He caught her wrist before she got more than a few steps away and moved around in front of her. "I'm not asking forgiveness for earlier. I'm not sorry for what I said or who I said it in front of. I'm asking forgiveness for what I'm about to do, because it might get me hit later."

Her gaze jerked to his. Her brow furrowed and her mouth opened, but Sebastian didn't give her a chance to utter the denial in her eyes. Instead, he used his purchase on her wrist to pull her toward him, scooped her up, and hauled her over his shoulder.

Christina shrieked in surprise, the sound echoing around the now quiet ballroom. "What on earth are you doing? Sebastian, you put me down this instant!"

"I will. Once we get outside." Ignoring the stares of the few people still left, he strode for the exit. "I told you we were going to talk. I just didn't tell you where."

She pounded his back with a fist. "You put me down right now or so help me."

He chuckled as he turned the corner and strode for the elevators at the other end of the long hallway. They passed several couples lingering, who all smiled and snickered. "Or so help you what? I've got you on your head. What, exactly, do you plan to do about it, Tina?"

True to her stubborn nature, she growled low in her throat. "Ohhhh, when I get my hands on you."

He stopped in front of the elevators and pushed the button. As he waited, the reflection in the mirrored doors caught his attention. Christina McKenzie's fine, sweet ass was front and center and wiggling in his face. Somehow, he'd have to resist that this weekend. If he wanted to truly earn her trust, he had to learn to control his desire. Prove to her she meant more to him than just a good lay.

"You can hit me later. I'll even hold still, but you've been putting me off for the last month, and I'm not taking no for an answer this time. We need to talk."

This time, she let out a helpless sigh. "Sebastian, please,

I'm in a dress, and I'm not wearing panties. People behind us can probably see all my parts."

Sebastian froze. For a moment, desire overrode everything else, and his pulse thundered in his ears. He stifled a groan. Of all the things for her to tell him, it had to be that.

The elevator dinged open, and he took a moment to get on and pushed the button for the ground floor. Some part of him insisted he was pushing boundaries, but neither could he resist sliding his palm over the curve of her delicious backside. "Feel that, sweetheart? That's your ass."

He followed her skirt to where the hem stopped, then dipped beneath it and slid his fingers along the seam. God. Her sleek, bare thighs were smooth as butter.

His resolve slipped another notch. Damned if he could stop himself from allowing his fingers to slip between her thighs, simply for the desperate need to feel her response. "*This* is the end of your skirt."

"Baz, please." She went limp on his shoulder, her voice a whisper in the quiet whir of the elevator motor.

This time, she got him. Her plea caressed over him. His cock thickened behind his fly. He gritted his teeth. *Shit. Don't do it. Whatever you do, don't do it. You're here to talk, not play.*

The need to discover the truth—whether or not she really was going commando—overwhelmed his brain. He slid his hand beneath her skirt, following the curve of her tight ass. He expected panties, and that she'd only been taunting him with that little tidbit. An attempt to get him to put her down maybe. His palm smoothed over warm, supple skin, though, and the knowledge settled over him. She really wasn't wearing any panties.

Christ.

"This is your ass." He followed the edge of one firm, supple cheek, dipping in between her thighs, allowing his fingers to graze her heat. The shiver that ran through her made his cock throb. He damn near dropped her for the desperate need to sink into her warmth. If he moved fast enough, could he make her come before they reached the ground floor? God how he ached to find out, just to hear the maddening little moan she made right before she tipped over the edge. "Nobody can see you, I promise."

He swallowed a curse, forced himself to pull his hand back, and reached down to adjust his erection. Thank God for long jackets. He had to have a freakin' tent by now.

He smacked her ass for good measure. "I'll put you down when we get to the car, so I know you won't run from me. If you wouldn't be so damn stubborn, I wouldn't need to do this."

She squirmed on his shoulder, twisting as if trying to look at him. "Me? How is this *my* fault?"

He blew out an exasperated breath. They weren't supposed to have this conversation until later. "A month, Tina. You've barely spoken to me for the last month. I get it. I really do. We crossed a line we can't go back from, but I hate that you don't trust me. So, I'm going to fix it."

Christina stilled on his shoulder again and went silent, but he could hear the wheels of her mind turning. Finally, her voice came as a quiet, almost reluctant murmur. "How?"

"You'll see."

The elevator ground to a halt and the doors dinged open. Sebastian ignored the overwhelming need to unload the emotion stuck in his chest and stepped out. That was a conversation they would eventually have, but right now, he needed to get her in the car. He wanted her alone when he said what he needed to say, and he wanted to be able to look her in the eyes when he said it. So she could see his and know he told her nothing but the truth.

As he moved down the quiet corridor to the lobby, people turned and gawked, but he set his sights on the black limo waiting at the curb. What mattered was the end destination. As he approached, Cade's driver, dressed in a formal black uniform, his white hair hidden beneath a black-rimmed cap, nodded in greeting and opened the back door. "Evening, sir."

Sebastian came to a stop at the edge of the sidewalk and nodded in return. "Evening, Daniel. Did he give you the address?"

"He did, sir." The driver winked, amusement sparking in the elderly man's eyes. "It's a lovely evening for a drive."

Clearly Cade had filled him in on the details. Sebastian could only shake his head.

"I sure hope so, Daniel. I sure hope so." As he set Christina to her feet, her body slid along his in the most delicious way. His cock twitched, pushing awkwardly and painfully against his zipper. Damn it. He couldn't even reach down and adjust the damn thing or the whole freakin' world would know. *Never mind me while I adjust the hard-on of the century.* His balls were probably blue by now.

He nodded at the open door behind her. "Please. Get in."

Christina huffed indignantly but didn't budge. Instead, she took her sweet time straightening and smoothing her skirt. "Sebastian, really. We're adults. There's no reason—"

Then and there, his last shred of patience snapped. He gripped her face in his hands and fused his lips to hers, effectively silencing her tirade. He shouldn't have done it, but her mouth was warm, and her body softened, leaning into him. Despite her anger, her lips opened beneath his assault, and her tongue flicked out to caress his. He was lost before he could blink.

Somehow managing to pull his wits about him, Sebastian forced himself to release her and jabbed a finger in the direction of the car interior. "Now get in the damn car before I pick you up and toss you in there."

She stuck her tongue out at him, an unladylike and childish gesture that made him smile in spite of himself, but finally climbed into the car.

He shoved a hand through his hair. "If I survive this weekend with my sanity intact, Daniel, it'll be a miracle."

Daniel smiled, amusement twinkling in his eyes. "Perhaps it'll be worth it in the end, sir."

Sebastian let out a quiet laugh. "From your mouth to God's ears."

Chapter Six

When Sebastian climbed into the car and settled into the seat beside her, Christina immediately stiffened. "Where are we going?"

She didn't bother to grace him with a glance in his direction, though. Rather, she turned to stare out the opposite window.

Sebastian sighed. He'd spent far too many years building walls between them. Breaking them down wouldn't be easy. "You'll see. I'd like it to be a surprise."

"If you're planning on seducing me, you might as well give up now, because I won't cave this time." Despite the boldness of her statement, she folded her arms over her stomach, her voice quiet in the space between them. "I think it's best if you leave this where it is."

He didn't know whether to laugh or scream. Given how he'd kissed her, he wasn't surprised to hear her say that, but he'd hoped somewhere inside she really did trust him. He released a heavy breath. He'd created this mess, and he had to get himself out of it. From now on, he had to be honest with her. No more holding back.

He scooted closer, until his hip bumped hers; then he scooped her up and deposited her onto his lap. She chirped in surprise, but he wrapped his arms around her, holding her firm. Not that she protested. He wanted to laugh. She put up a good fight, but when push came to shove, she always caved. That she did gave him hope.

He stroked her back, hoping touch would somehow ease the tension between them. "I'm not seducing you, though I'd be lying if I said I haven't thought about you naked beneath me all damn night. Never mind that I have memories of exactly that. Your soft body. The way you tremble when I touch you. God, you don't know what that does to me, and I'm not even sure I have the right words. But for the time being, I need you to believe that you could and will never be another notch on my bedpost. I said it earlier, and I'll keep saying it until you believe me."

She turned to stare out the window again. "Right. I'm special. Like I haven't heard *that* before."

He studied her profile with a heavy heart. It had always been fireworks between them, but her walls were higher than he'd anticipated. Who'd hurt her so much she put up such high walls to keep people out? Had *he* done this to her? Was this the result of pushing too hard to keep her at a safe distance? Whatever the reason, knowing someone had hurt her to that degree made his heart ache.

He stroked the backs of his fingers down her cheek. He

couldn't help touching her and his hands seemed to have a will of their own. "Yeah, actually, Tina, you are, which is why I've always kept my distance from you. There are two people in my life who mean the world to me, and I almost lost one of them recently because of my own stupid pride. You and Cade are family, about the only family I have left. So make no mistake about it. There's nothing casual about making love to you for me."

Then he waited. Being that honest with her had him shaking. His heart hammered an unsteady beat. He'd never done the *bare the soul* thing with anybody else. Sadly, not even with Jean. He liked his relationships light and playful. The less he became attached, the less people could leave him. It was a terrible way to live. Doing so left a lonely ache in the pit of his stomach that got to him in the dead of night.

Christina brought out the need in him, which was why he was always so irritable around her. He wanted her too damn much. Oh, being that way was childish for sure, of the grade school variety. Tease the girl you secretly have a crush on because it was easier than saying, "Hey, I like you." Putting up walls accomplished what he needed them to. If she was so pissed at him she couldn't think straight, she'd stop being everything he needed. If they never crossed that line, then he could keep her forever.

Except they had crossed that line, and he had two choices now. He could turn around and leave their relationship where it was…or try to fix the way she saw him. Losing his father had changed his view of his world. He'd meant so little to the old man his father had literally left him nothing but more "you'll never be good enough" demands. He needed to fix his relationship with Christina.

She didn't say anything for so long that knots began to form on the knots already tangled in his stomach. Tension mounted in the interior of the limo like a living, breathing entity. Finally, the stiff set of her shoulders softened, and she turned her head, meeting his gaze. "Then why are we here?"

He set his hand in her lap, palm up. "Because I hate when you're angry with me. You have all these wrong ideas about me and it bugs the shit out of me. I told you that morning. Letting you believe what you wanted about me created distance."

She looked down at his hand but kept hers in her lap. "Why now?"

He sighed and pulled his hand back. "Because I hate that you think I could ever use you that way. I hate you think I'm even capable of using any woman like they're little more than a warm body. I don't treat women like that. I never have. I may not like commitment, but I don't believe in treating people the way my father treated me. I've let you believe what you wanted, because it was safer. I hate it when you mother me for the same reason. Because a really big part of me needs it."

She darted a glance at him and rolled her eyes. "You and Caden. I swear. I do not mother you. I *care* for you. There's a difference. I happen to enjoy taking care of the people I hold dear to me."

Her choice of words lodged themselves in his heart. At the very least, she cared about him. That had to be a good sign. "Exactly. Nobody but the damn servants has ever shown me that kind of caring."

The last edge of stiffness left her shoulders, but the wary edge remained in her eyes.

He trailed his fingertips up the side of her arm, enjoying the suppleness of her skin. Sitting in his lap like this, she was damn distracting. With the partition up between them and the driver, they were relatively alone back here, and God how he wanted her. That she wasn't wearing panties taunted him. A little shift of their clothing and they could be shuddering in bliss before they reached the lake.

It was the feel of her there that got to him, though, and the truth bubbled out before he could stop the words from leaving his tongue.

"I was raised by a man who went through five wives and the only care he ever showed for me was whether or not I lived up to his lousy ideal. Despite everything I've accomplished, I was still a disappointment to him when he died. So, I don't know if I can be what you need, if I'm built for committing myself to one woman or even if I believe it's possible. I tried once and all I did was end up hurting her."

Christina nodded and turned her gaze out her window. "Jean was good for you. You never called her your girlfriend, though. You never brought her over for Christmas or Thanksgiving. You never talked much about her at all."

Memories rose in his mind, leaving the bitter taste of regret in his mouth. His chest filled with the all too familiar aching emptiness. He'd hurt Jean. He hadn't meant to, but he had. He still hadn't forgiven himself, either. She was a good woman, and she'd deserved better. "Mmm. I tried with her, I honestly did, but I couldn't be what she needed, no matter how much I wanted to."

He hooked two fingers beneath her chin, turned her head, and pressed a soft kiss to her lips, then set her back on the seat beside him. If he didn't, he was going to seduce her out of that silky dress right there in the limo. Which would get him all of nowhere. This weekend wasn't about sex. "And to answer your question, we're here because I'd like you to spend the weekend with me. I want you to see *me*, not what you think you see. Though whether you stay with me this weekend is entirely up to you."

"You kidnapped me, but I get a choice?" She arched a brow at him, cynical, but the corners of her mouth twitched, betraying her.

His patience snapped. He rolled his eyes right back at her and dragged a hand through his hair. "You're making me nuts. Do you know that? You are really making me work for this. I don't know what I want more right now, to kiss your sassy mouth until you give in, or turn the car around and take you home. Do you do this with every guy or am I just special?"

Christina didn't respond the way he'd anticipated. Instead of the fight she usually gave, her gaze dropped from his. The same fierce woman who always stood her ground and poked him in the chest deflated. Her shoulders rounded, melancholy hanging on her, so palpable his chest ached. "You're just special."

Her voice drifted into the space between them barely

above a murmur, but she might as well have shouted the words. They had the same impact her bomb had the morning she'd barged into his condo and announced she was in love with him.

He banged his head back against the seat. Damn it all to hell. There went all his good intentions.

He slid from the seat and knelt on the floor in front of her. She turned her head, her eyes wide with wary and alarm. He slid his hands up the tops of her thighs, allowed himself a moment to luxuriate in the incredible creaminess of her skin. She had baby-soft skin, so smooth he wanted to wrap himself up in her. How she achieved such suppleness, he didn't know, but he was damn grateful for the effort.

"W-what are you doing?" Her voice trembled, those eyes filling with a tangible heat.

He stroked the skin on the insides of her thighs, delighting in the shiver that ran through her. "I'm *trying* to let this be your choice. I'm *trying* to be honest and let you come to me, but I can't stand it. There's only so much a man can take."

He hooked his hands beneath her knees and yanked, pulling her ass to the edge of the seat. Her thighs parted. Her skirt rode dangerously high. God, plunging into her silky heat would be so easy, just a little shift of clothing. He ached to make love to her until she curled herself around him.

He ignored the desire, set his hands on the seat on either side of her, and leaned in, until he took every breath with her. He rubbed the erection pulsing to life in his pants against the heat of her, teasing her. Showing her what she did to him.

She gasped, and her breathing hitched. Despite her need to keep her distance, her hips arched into his, her pelvis rocking into the intimate connection, grinding against his cock. "Baz, please."

He skimmed his lips over her stubborn chin, across her jaw to her ear, tasting any part of her she'd allow. "You make me crazy. I don't have pretty words, Tina. I wish I did, but I don't. I can't believe you've never caught on to how I feel about you, because sometimes it's all I can think about. The more crap life throws at me, the more I crave everything about you that makes you who you are."

He worked his way back to her mouth and brushed his lips over hers. When he pulled back, she followed, a little huff of breath leaving her lips. He allowed himself a taste, the soft tangle of his lips with hers.

"You barge into my apartment at eight damn o'clock in the morning and insist on making me breakfast. You're stubborn as hell and you don't back down. When you stand up and poke me in the chest, all I can think is how much I want to grab that finger and pull you in. Do you have any idea how many hard-ons I've had to hide from you?"

She stared at him, tenderness gleaming from those liquid eyes, capturing him in the time it took him to draw his next breath. Only one woman made him this vulnerable. Her.

"For years, I've swallowed my feelings for you and shoved them down. You're my best friend's sister and guys don't go there." Never mind that if he ever lost her his world would come screeching to a halt. "You *are* different, whether you want to hear it or not."

He brushed his mouth over hers, the lightest of kisses. Her eyes closed, her lips opening beneath his. His erection, caught between their bodies and throbbing against the seam of his pants, rubbed her mound. She moaned and arched against him, but Sebastian forced himself to pull back.

He ignored his body's urging and slid onto the seat beside her instead. Turning his gaze out the window, he tried desperately not to focus on the painful throbbing of his cock. "If you really don't want to spend the weekend with me, I get it. I'm not sure I'd blame you. You've got this image of me I purposely set, because it kept you at a safe distance, but I'm done. I'm done pretending you don't mean anything to me, that you're just my best friend's sister. Because you aren't. You want to know the truth? That's it."

He dared a glance at her. Her chest rose and fell at a rapid pace, but Christina hadn't moved an inch. She sat staring out her window, looking wanton and half fucked, with her legs spread, skirt barely covering the tops of her thighs. His hands itched to stroke over those luscious limbs, to luxuriate in her silky skin, to dive between and stroke her to orgasm. By God she was beautiful in the throes of passion, and he had the unbearable desire to know how wet she was.

He kept his hands to himself. This had to be her choice, so for the time being, until he knew her answer, he'd ignore the lusciousness seated beside him. Instead, he jerked his gaze to his own window, idly watching the trees and buildings blur past. "I would, however, like you to spend the weekend with me. I want you to know *me*. All of me."

An unbearable silence passed between them. He waited

on the edge of a precipice for her to react, to say…some-thing. Anything. His shoulders ached, his thighs stiffened, his feet braced on the floorboards, and his gut churned. She shifted in the seat beside him, straightening, but didn't say anything for so long he counted the seconds. When he got to thirty, his hands curled along the seat's edge, short nails biting into the soft leather. No woman had ever mattered the way she did, and his every muscle sat poised as he waited.

"Okay."

She offered the word on a trembling whisper, but she might as well have shouted it. Heart pounding a giddy beat from the vicinity of his throat, he jerked his gaze to hers. She was staring at him, her gaze full of a mix of curiosity and ten-derness. *His* Christina had come back. No longer angry and mistrustful, the tender, caring side of her he loved so much had returned. She'd let down her walls.

"I have to admit what you want has merit. You're right. You do seem different, and I *would* like to get to know you without the walls. I have for a while if I'm honest."

What had to be a stupid grin plastered itself across his face. He felt like a kid having asked a girl out for the first time and realizing she'd actually said yes. His heart had pounded as hard back then, too.

"Thank you." He reached across the seat and held his hand out, palm up. This time, she threaded her fingers with his.

They occasionally made small talk. Christina attempting to pry his surprise out of him. Work. Occasionally the weather. It surprised the hell out of him how simple and yet so profound holding hands with a woman could be. She'd relaxed and an air of intimacy filled the interior of the limo. The time passed in comfortable silence. He'd never been this close to her before. He almost hated to see the ride end.

Thirty minutes or so later, the car inched up the driveway and came to a stop in front of the familiar house. The place belonged to her family. It sat at the end of a small private road and the backside led out onto the beach. It had spectacular views of Lake Washington and enough privacy they would be alone but not isolated.

"The cabin." Christina turned her head, awe in her voice and in her eyes. "This is your surprise? Why here?"

Sebastian climbed from the car and held out his hand, waiting until she stepped onto the blacktop beside him. When she took his hand, he threaded their fingers and turned to eye the house. Two stories high, the place was made of natural wooden logs, beautifully built, luxurious but with a distinct rough-around-the edges feel. It was perfect.

"I thought about one of the resorts. We have one up here on Lake Washington, but it seemed cheesy. I wanted somewhere we could be alone. Unfortunately, my father sold ours years ago, so I asked Cade for a favor. He gave me the keys and helped me make sure the place would be cleaned and stocked."

"Ah. So that's how you pulled this off. I should have known Caden would play your partner in crime in this."

She stiffened beside him, her face falling. Something heavy clearly weighed on her mind.

He tugged on her hand. "Say it. No more holding back."

She turned to look at him, face solemn, fear written in her eyes. "You still have a date."

He couldn't help but smile. He'd gotten so caught up in her he'd forgotten to let her off the hook. "Only with you. I'm surprised you didn't recognize Stacy. She's Cade's newest hire. In exchange for making sure nobody outbid her, I'm giving her a week at one of the resorts."

Her body relaxed, her eyes searching his face. Finally, her brows knit together in concern. "I'm sorry your father sold your cabin. Was it because of your mother?"

He turned back to the house. The familiar memory rose unbidden and the same tightness clenched at his chest. It was bittersweet. He treasured and loathed with equal measure the memories he had of his family's cabin. He remembered his mother's smile. The smell of the cookies she baked floating through the house. He remembered, too, the way his parents had fought, all the yelling and crying. They'd fought a lot toward the end. "Mmm. He sold the house a few years after she left. Said he couldn't stand being there anymore."

Christina squeezed his hand. "I'm sorry."

He shrugged, attempting for offhanded and dismissive, attempting to drive back the painful memories rising over him. All those summers. He wished like hell he didn't, but he remembered every damn one of them. He would never forget the sound of his mother's laughter. Or the anger in her voice the day she left.

"I couldn't blame him for wanting to get rid of the place. After all, that's where it all went down. They had the argument of the century, and she stormed from the house and never came back. No divorce papers. No goodbyes. As hurt as I was, I always imagined he hated her more than I did. Truth is, I didn't want the place, either." He tugged on her hand. "Come on. Let's go inside."

He reached into his pockets and pulled out the keys. Daniel moved around the end of the car to get the bags from the trunk.

One step through the door, they both halted dead in their tracks on the welcome mat. What seemed a full minute passed in silence as they stared at the space spread out before them. The damn cabin looked like the Valentine section of the grocery store had exploded. Red and white candles covered every available surface. On the counters in the kitchen. On the fireplace mantel in the living room. Bouquets of red flowers dotted the countertops. A bottle of champagne sat in a bucket of ice on the island counter separating the kitchen from the living area. The pièce de résistance, though? A trail of red rose petals leading to the staircase. He had no desire to follow them.

Daniel stepped up behind them. "Where to, sir?"

Sebastian turned sideways, moving out of the way of the door. He wanted to tell the man to leave them, that he'd carry them himself, but Daniel was a proud man. So he simply nodded in the direction of the staircase. "The bedrooms, I suppose, please."

"Yes, sir." Daniel smiled and nodded politely, then moved past them, carrying their small bags toward the staircase, hidden along the far wall beside the enormous stone fireplace.

Five minutes later, Daniel left and Sebastian and Christina stood side by side at the edge of the living room. As the limo purred to life outside, Christina turned her head and arched an amused brow, one corner of her mouth quirking upward. "I thought you said you didn't bring me here to seduce me?"

"I didn't." He dragged a hand through his hair and swallowed hard as he took in the space. If this was Cade's idea of a joke, Sebastian wasn't laughing. Though, if he knew Cade, all this damn romancey stuff was a blatant shove.

Christina's eyes flashed in challenge. "What happened to honesty, Baz?"

He held up his hands in surrender and let out a nervous laugh.

"Oh, don't look at me. This has Cade written *all* over it." When she narrowed her gaze on him, he dropped his hands, his smile melting from his face. "You don't plan to make this easy on me, do you?"

The corners of her mouth twitched, but to her credit, Christina didn't budge an inch. Damn stubborn woman.

"I thought you said you were done hiding from me?" She waved a flippant hand in the air, a sort of la-di-da gesture. "Or was that lovely speech in the car lip service?"

The last of Sebastian's willpower snapped. He closed the distance between them, backed her against the wall adjacent to the door, and set his hands on either side of her. His face sat inches from hers, her mouth now close enough her warm breaths puffed against his lips like a goddamn lure.

Her breathing increased, chest rising and falling at a more rapid pace. Good.

"You want honest, baby? No, I didn't bring you here to seduce you. Despite the looks of this place, and I am going to *kill* Cade, I had the best of intentions. Now that we're alone, however, my cock aches. I want to hike that dress up around your waist and fuck you against this wall. Telling me you're not wearing panties was the wrong thing to do if you want to keep me at a distance." He straightened and dragged a hand through his hair. In frustration. In barely contained desire. More than a little frazzled, he turned his head and cocked a brow at her. "Is that honest enough for you?"

She sagged back against the wall, once again the soft, feminine woman who called to something primal within him. "I love when you talk to me that way. As long as we're being honest, I find it awfully difficult to resist you, too, when you say things like that."

Just that fast, his irritation flitted away and one corner of his mouth hitched. He chuckled and leaned in, pressing his body into the softness of hers, and brushed a kiss across her alluring mouth. "You are the most mixed up woman I know."

She arched into him, her tongue flicking against his bottom lip, and shook her head. Her hands slid down his chest to his belt buckle. "You aren't the only one who hides, Baz, or whose been trying to keep this on the straight and narrow. But if you want honesty, you never talk to me like that, and it's addicting. You treat me like a kid sister, and I've spent years wishing you'd see me as a woman."

Buckle out of the way, she made fast work of the button

and zipper on his slacks, then slid her hand inside his boxers. Her warm fingers curled around his cock, and Sebastian squeezed his eyes shut. Everything about Christina had always been soft. Her hands were no exception, sliding around him like warm silk.

He clenched his jaw until his teeth ached. "Shit. Easy, baby. Please. I'm so far past the edge."

Her body left his, but he was shaking too hard, his desire ramped up too high, to pry open his eyes to figure out where she'd gone. Two seconds later, her warm mouth enveloped the head of his penis, answering the question. Shocked by the velvet of her tongue sliding along his length, Sebastian opened his eyes and looked down. It was a fucking fantasy come to life. Christina McKenzie was on her knees at his feet, sucking his cock into her mouth.

As if that weren't enough, she peered up at him around her mouthful, working his cock like she owned him. That hard edge had returned to her gaze. She was once again the take-charge CEO, the woman who'd barged into his apartment and demanded he eat breakfast or she'd tie him to a chair.

A heated tremor moved through him. He braced his hands on the wall over her head. *Shit. Shit, shit, shit.* This side of her was sexy as hell. His fucking knees were shaking. She had him on the edge of release, no doubt exactly where she wanted him.

She wasn't taking any prisoners, either. She sucked hard on the tip, making his eyes roll back in his head with the intense, sudden rush of pleasure, and popped him from her mouth. Then she swirled her tongue over the head like she'd done it a thousand times and knew exactly where he liked to be stroked. "Let it go, Baz."

He didn't have it in him to argue. He closed his eyes, dropped his head in abandon, and reached out blindly to thread his fingers into her silky hair. He held on for dear life, gently rocking his hips into her velvet mouth. "You're a goddess, Tina, you know that? A fucking goddess. Oh, Christ, baby, I won't last if you keep that up."

Apparently, she wasn't listening. Her warm mouth slid along his length, taking him deep, and pleasure shot to the tips of his toes. Sebastian groaned, locked his knees, and planted his feet to keep from crumbling. His balls drew tight against his body and the tingle began at the base of his spine. He might as well have been an inexperienced kid all over again. He was at the mercy of a woman who knew how to drive him out of his freaking mind.

She was relentless, her rhythm increasing with every glide of her soft lips along his length, sucking him harder and deeper. Of all things he'd ever imagined her doing to him, he'd fantasized about this one a lot over the years. The reality was a damn cliché…so far better than anything he'd ever imagined. Her mouth was hot and silky, and the soft purring emanating from her throat only increased the ache in his balls. She sounded like she enjoyed what she did, and the sound of her satisfaction set him ablaze.

Half a dozen strokes of her luscious mouth had his orgasm rushing up at blinding speed. With a strangled moan, he gave himself over to her, emptying himself into her hot, inviting mouth.

By the time the luscious spasms finally released him, he was shaking from head to toe. He had enough coherence to haul her off the floor; then he wrapped his arms around her and leaned into her, burying his face in her throat. He needed her as close as possible.

He hadn't a clue how to tell her that. He could seduce women as easily as breathing, but Christina was different and the right words never seemed to be there when he needed them. Now was one of those times. He needed her to know how incredible she was, but the right words eluded him.

When he finally lifted his head, anxiousness rose in her eyes. For a moment they searched his before she drew a breath and released it. "If we're going to do this, I have rules."

He playfully rolled his eyes. "Of course you do."

She hiked her chin a notch, but he didn't miss the way her gaze danced over his. "For now, this is only for the weekend. I can't promise you any more than that. And no emotions. I know you, Baz. I've watched you leave a trail of broken hearts in your wake, whether you mean to or not. I don't want to be one of them."

She stopped, swallowed hard, and turned her gaze to the floor. She drew a deep breath, blew it out, and looked down. Her fingers toyed with the top button of his shirt. "I also know you need to get married in order to fulfill your father's will."

The sudden mention took him by surprise. Her clear nervousness had alarm skittering along his spine. She looked like she had something she was afraid to tell him. Christina

McKenzie wasn't afraid of anything. Where was she going with this?

"Yes."

She lifted her gaze to his. "I also won't marry you."

Okay, he had to admit it. That stung.

He drew back, folding his arms across his chest. Now he had to know the truth. "Good, because I wasn't going to ask. Might I ask why not, though?"

Her face blanked. An expression he'd seen one time too many over the years. She was shutting him out, putting up the exact wall she'd demanded they take down.

She stepped sideways, sliding away from him, and shook her head. "Because I won't."

He caught her wrist, refusing to allow her to retreat too far, and pinned her with a hard stare. He repeated his question more firmly this time. "Why?"

Her gaze jerked to his, alarm written in her widened eyes. Then her mouth formed a thin line. She yanked her hand from his and turned her back to him. "No."

"Say it, Christina." He knew a lot of things about her, but one thing he'd figured out only recently was she'd lied. She liked when he called her Tina. It was his pet name for her. Despite what she'd told him a month ago, she hated when he called her Christina. He was usually upset when he did and hurt always flashed through her gaze when he said it. "You want honesty from me? You have to be willing to give it as well. Tell me what you're thinking."

She whirled around to face him. The tears that filled her eyes cut up his insides, but he had a feeling she was making a point and he needed to know what it was.

"I'm a forever kind of girl, Baz. If I ever marry you..." She stopped, swallowed hard, her voice wobbling. "If I ever marry you, it's going to be for forever. Not a year or until you decide you're bored with me. And it's going to be because you love me, too. I love you too much to settle for less."

She turned and stalked away, moving in the direction of the staircase. He let her go. He was pretty sure they both needed a moment to recover, because her words sank over him, settling into his bones, into all those painful places. Christina loved him like *that*. Not a simple love or a love easily dismissed, but the hard kind. Where you made sacrifices for the one you loved and made them gladly, sometimes even to the detriment of yourself.

The funny part was, she had no idea he *did* love her like that.

In that moment, he knew two things. Despite being honest with her, she still didn't trust him. Hell. He wasn't sure he could trust himself not to screw this up, the way he had with Jean.

He also knew that when this weekend was over, he had a big decision to make. Namely, was he really ready to lay his heart on the line? To fully commit himself to her and be hers and only hers? Was he ready to finally take the first step into moving beyond the legacy his father had left and finding his own happiness? He'd have to put their relationship on the line.

He'd have to risk losing her.

Chapter Seven

Christina stared for a moment into the familiar room. She'd ended up in what had always been her and Caden's bedroom whenever their family vacationed here at Lake Washington. They'd had this cabin since she and Caden were young. Like Sebastian, they'd spent quite a few summers here.

The house wasn't overly huge. Seated on the edge of the beach, it had gorgeous views of the lake and a private boat ramp. The bedrooms took up the top floor. With oak-finished wood-beam walls, handmade quilts, and a night-stand made from an old tree stump, the room—and the house itself—had a rustic, homey feel. Her parents' idea of "roughing it," of course, was no room service and meals they had to make themselves. The master bedroom contained the ginormous king bed, topped with a similar handmade quilt, and no doubt covered in more of the rose petals.

She rolled her eyes but couldn't stop her smile. Sebastian

was right. That particular gesture, along with the red and white candles scattered throughout the house, screamed of Caden. Sebastian didn't appear to have a romantic bone in his body. Out of all the women she'd seen him with over the years, she'd never seen him give any of them flowers. He'd always had a flare for the playful and mischievous. Caden was the one more prone to grand gestures.

She sighed into the empty room. She should never have allowed Sebastian to bring her here, should never have agreed to this weekend with him. It wasn't like her. At all. She hadn't decided yet if she truly wanted the dream. The kids. The husband. The house. What she craved in the dead of night, when the loneliness ate away at her need to be self-sufficient, was something simpler. She wanted a man who'd worship her the way Caden worshiped Hannah. The way her father worshipped her mother. She'd never been a romantic person. Being at the top of her class, her studies had always come first, which suited her father fine.

Caden's romantic display at the bachelor auction last year had done her in. Christina wanted, more than anything, for someone to make that kind of gesture for her.

She'd always dreamed Sebastian would be the one. The silly schoolgirl's dream had stuck. Cinderella had always drawn the part of her that was, as Caden often put it, overwhelmingly girl.

So, why the hell was she here?

She sank onto the bed on the right, lay back, and closed her eyes. Every bone in her body weighted with a sudden, overwhelming exhaustion. The truth beat behind her breastbone along to the thud of her heartbeat, strong and undeniable. She'd come because she couldn't help herself. Sebastian's touch was her kryptonite. In the car, he'd set her in his lap and wrapped his arms around her. God how she loved the simple bliss of being held against his strong chest, encompassed in his scent. When he'd actually gotten down on his knees in front of her and rubbed his erection against her, she'd almost caved and begged him to fuck her right there.

Mostly, she'd come because she'd allowed herself to hope. She needed to find out for herself if he truly meant what he'd told her.

The bed dipped, the old springs creaking in protest. Christina's heart skipped, and her eyes popped open. On his hands and knees, Sebastian climbed onto the bed, rising over her. He settled between her thighs, holding himself on his elbows. The delicious weight of him effectively pinned her to the mattress. His heat infused hers and his luscious scent, all male and all Sebastian, swirled around her like a lure.

Somewhere over the last few minutes, he'd lost his jacket, and his hair fell over his forehead, giving him a rumpled but altogether alluring appearance. He could look so boyish sometimes, and it was a damn good look on him.

His heavy-lidded gaze settled on hers, full of a lethal combination of arousal and determination. "I have a few demands of my own."

She nodded. It was only fair. "All right."

"First one, no more walls. For this weekend, I'd like us to be honest with each other. That means you don't get to run from me or hold anything back. No matter what it is." He stroked the hair back off her face, the tip of his right index finger brushing the skin behind her ear. "I won't make you any promises I can't keep if you'll let me in."

His nearness, his tender touch, the husky tone of his voice, made her shiver. Her breathing hitched. This was the side of him she couldn't resist. The heart of the man.

"That goes both ways." She longed to bend her knees, to cradle his hips. He was mightily aroused. His cock lay hard and heavy behind the seam of his pants, and she ached to adjust her position in order to settle him more intimately against her. An inch down and to the right and the head of his cock would nudge her clit in the most delicious way...

"Exactly my point. All I want is to earn your trust. The way you looked at me before you left the room..." He shook his head and stroked his fingers through her hair again. "I hate it when you look at me like that."

The regret rising in his eyes had something more than desire settling between them. That dark heaviness she'd noted in the limo returned. Sebastian could be broody when he wanted to be. She longed, more than she wanted to tell him, to know this part of him. Talking with him, getting to hold him, filled a part of her heart she couldn't let go of. He didn't show this side of himself often and God help her, she wanted more. She wanted all of *him*.

She shook her head, her stomach turning in confusion. "I—"

Sebastian brushed his mouth over hers, silencing her protest before the words could leave her mouth.

"You don't trust me, and I can't blame you. I can't change

my past or the places I've been, but I hate that all I've managed to do is hurt you." His gaze flitted over her face, searching for a moment before he leaned his forehead against hers. Those hypnotic blue eyes pleaded with her. "I'd never do anything to purposely hurt you. Somewhere deep inside, you have to know that."

She closed her eyes, her heartbeat ratcheting up a notch. God, he had to go and say that. She knew damn well Sebastian might be a lot of things, but he'd never been a cruel man. After all, Spike had been a homeless cat he'd lured off the street with basic things like compassion and a gentle touch. He'd taken the time to earn the cat's trust. So, yes, she knew damn well Sebastian would never *purposely* hurt anybody.

She opened her eyes. The worry and palpable regret in his wrapped around her and sank deep. If she made it out of this weekend with her heart intact, it would be a miracle. This might well be a suicide mission.

"I do know, but the effect is still the same. You don't know if you can truly be what I need, and I don't know if I want to take the risk of ending up like Jean. I'm agreeing to this not because I think it's wise or even because I agree with your little mission, though I think it's sweet you want to earn my trust." She stroked a hand up his back, enjoying the solid press of the muscle, the warmth of his body. "I've long suspected there's a heart inside this chest somewhere."

"Then why are you here?"

She sighed. She'd promised him honesty. "Because I can't resist you, either. You touch me and my body melts."

"Shit." Sebastian's eyes slid shut, a tremor running

through him. "Wrong thing to tell me if you're trying to keep me at arm's length, sweetheart. I've been aroused since you were in my lap in the limo, never mind what you did downstairs. Lying with you like this is killing me."

For a moment, Christina could only stare at him. His struggle moved across his face, his brow furrowed, his mouth falling open as he released a serrated breath. The last of her resolve deserted her. *This.* This was why she'd allowed him to talk her into coming. He trembled in her arms, as if her words and her touch did the same thing to him his did to her, and the power of it was intoxicating.

Unable to resist touching him any longer, she lifted her head and molded her lips to the curve of his jaw. She allowed herself to taste his skin, to revel in the rough scrape of his five o'clock shadow against her lips. She wanted to commit every tiny moment with him to memory. Her resolve to save her heart be damned. She needed him, too. "We're in agreement, then?"

Whatever reservations had been between them evaporated. He rocked his hips into hers, groaned long and low, and buried his face in her throat. He feasted on her, nipping and sucking at her skin, over the curve of her shoulder, up the side of her neck and the edge of her jaw. One hand wandered her curves, from the side of her hip to her ass, squeezing gently. "Yes. Christ, yes. For now. Are we done talking, baby?"

She couldn't help the quiet laugh that escaped her and nipped at his jaw. "You're cranky when you're aroused, Sebastian."

He lifted his head, worry once again rising in his searching eyes. "I'm sorry. I need you. It's been a rough month. I want to bury myself so damn deep in your sweetness I can't tell where you end and I begin, and I don't want to come out until sometime Sunday."

"Then what are you waiting for?" She leaned in and raked her teeth over his earlobe. "Fuck me, Sebastian."

He groaned, low and deep, and opened his eyes. The heat within them scorched her from the inside out.

"I'd never imagined you'd have such a dirty mouth." He grinned, his eyes twinkling with amusement. "Say it again."

He dipped his head, his lips skimming her body, leaving a trail of fire in their wake. Down her neck. Across her shoulder. Between her breasts. Above the neckline of her dress. Everywhere he touched came alive. Another wave of heated shivery goose bumps ran the surface of her skin. Her eyes closed. When he planted a soft kiss at the top of her solar plexus, she gasped, her body bowing off the bed.

"Say it again, sweetheart. Tell me what you want."

The seductive rumble of his voice against her body sent a wave of heat straight to her core. Sebastian in seduction mode was a powerful force indeed.

Her fingers curled into the quilt beneath her, fisting the soft material. "I want you to fuck me, Baz. Hard."

He let out a sound that was half groan, half frustrated growl as he moved down her body. He planted a series of kisses down her stomach, his breath warm through the thin silk of her dress, his hands caressing, stroking, teasing. As he settled between her legs, his warm palms slid up the insides, setting her thighs to trembling. "I've thought about this for years. Lying between your silky thighs. Getting to push one of your damn skirts up past your waist, so I could see you. All of you."

His comment caught her. Deciding she had to know, she furrowed her brow but didn't open her eyes. "What's the matter with my skirts?"

Quiet laughter rumbled out of him. His thumbs stroked the insides of her thighs, grazing her outer lips. "Out of all the things I said, you focus on why I hate your skirts? It's because they hug your fantastic ass. Your skirts give me hard-ons."

His warm breath whispered over her flesh as he bent his head to her mound. He inhaled softly, then groaned again.

"God, you smell good." His hot tongue flicked out, the tip following the seam of her slit, teasing her already aroused flesh. "I've wanted to taste you for a long time."

She squeezed her eyes shut. Tiny tremors ran through her body. Sebastian had her on the edge of a heightened state of arousal, but an ultra-vulnerable ache gripped her chest that had her trembling for an entirely different reason. She didn't know how to tell him, or even if she should. She'd had a lot of lovers over the years, but none ever attempted to recipro-cate when she'd given oral sex, and she'd never asked. The act was intimate and accepting made her vulnerable.

She reached down, attempting to pull him back up. "I'd rather you fuck me."

He caught her hand in his, pinning it to the bed, and leaned in again, skimming his mouth over her lips. "Uh-uh.

You had your way with me downstairs. Now it's my turn."

Pleasure slid to her toes. Her limbs began to quake in earnest, but her chest clenched with the fear of letting go. She'd never been this vulnerable with any man. She took charge on purpose.

She squeezed his fingers, reaching down with the other hand to pull at him. "Baz, please..."

His movements paused, his gaze burning into her, but she couldn't bring herself to open her eyes or look at him.

"Has anybody ever done this for you before?" Disbelief laced his gentle tone.

Her face heated to a thousand degrees. What the hell did she tell him? That he was the only man who'd ever offered? That she'd always accepted that was the way it would be?

When she didn't answer, Sebastian made a sound of displeasure in the back of his throat. Then his thumbs caressed her flesh, stroking the outsides of her nether lips, and his hot breath blew over her, cooling her heated skin. "Then it's about time someone did. I'm honored it's me."

A heated shiver shot through her, but the ultra-vulnerable sensation wouldn't release her or let her relax. Here, like this, she was at his mercy.

She turned her head, the heat in her face increasing. She might as well be a damn virgin. "Baz..."

He stroked a hand up her stomach, his fingers sweeping her left nipple, tight and extended with arousal. "Shhh. Relax. It's only me, Tina. Let me pleasure you."

He didn't wait for her answer but slid his hands up her thighs, pushing her dress farther up until it settled around her waist. Every muscle tightened as her body sat poised on the edge, waiting for the first intimate touch.

She didn't know what she'd expected from him or the exchange, but the first tender stroke of his tongue had her melting into the mattress. His tongue was hot, his breath cool against her moist flesh. His soft strokes, the way his warm, smooth palms continually stroked her body, had her reservations evaporating one by one.

He nuzzled her mound with his nose and mouth, stroked her nether lips with his fingers, his touch always tender. Sebastian took the act slowly, taking his time to caress her, to build her arousal all over again. Hands braced on the insides of her thighs, holding her open, he didn't charge in. He dipped in, caressing her with the tip of his tongue or giving her a long, tender stroke and an occasional light butterfly flick.

Her breath caught. She forgot her protests altogether, and her clit throbbed, begging for release. Her hands fisted in the quilt beneath her as she held on against the onslaught. Oh God, he was good at this. Every luscious stroke built her up, had her firmly seated on the edge of release. A final flick of his tongue shoved her over the edge. Her orgasm flooded through her, a luxurious, bone-melting rush of liquids. Her toes curled. Her back arched off the bed. "Sebastian!"

He didn't stop there. As she came down from the high, he continued to stroke her, licking softly, sucking her clit into his mouth. Too sensitive post-orgasm, the flicks of his tongue bordered between pain and extreme pleasure. She attempted to close her legs, to push him away, but he refused to relent. He pushed her legs flat, holding her wide open.

He buried his face in her heat, nipping, sucking, and licking at her with an abandon that awed her. All the while, he moaned against her flesh. His audible enjoyment sent subtle vibrations through her sensitive clit like the buzz of a vibrator. Another orgasm struck like a lightning bolt. This one scorched her from the inside out. Every muscle went rigid, tightening and loosening in a hot rush. Her scream caught in her throat, leaving her mouth as little more than a strangled gasp.

When she collapsed back into the bed, spent and exhausted and panting, he freed her limbs. He laid his head on her thigh, fingers stroking the insides. Long moments passed as she lay there, eyes closed, trying to catch her breath. She couldn't stop shaking. Aftershocks, some experienced part of her suggested. She'd never been so vulnerable with a man before, and the aftereffects had her brain scrambled and her limbs quaking.

Sebastian moved up beside her and gathered her to him, wrapping both arms tightly around her. She settled against the warmth and strength of his familiar body. She wasn't the only one affected by the exchange, either. His heart beat an erratic rhythm beneath her ear. His chest rose and fell at a rapid pace, his breath sawing in and out of his mouth as hard as hers, and his body shook against her side.

He kissed the top of her head, his voice a husky rumble beneath her ear. "You okay?"

She didn't know how to answer that question. How could she possibly tell him what he'd done for her? He'd given her something no man ever had, and she had to admit, she felt closer to him for it. So she hugged him tighter, buried her face in the warmth of his chest, and inhaled his familiar scent, needing both to root her. "Th-that was incredible, but I c-can't stop sh-shaking."

He stroked her hair with one hand, tightening his hold on her with the other. "Good. Sleep."

She tipped her head back, seeking out his gaze. "But w-what about you?"

For a moment, he didn't say anything but simply stared. There, in the tiny space, something moved between them, unspoken but every bit as powerful as the pull of the moon to the tide. It settled deep inside, unmistakable and satisfying and terrifying all rolled in one tumultuous tangle of emotion.

A connection. The luscious pull of intimacy shared.

She'd been here before. The relationship hadn't worked out, of course, but she knew what this moment meant. It was a moment of realization, when the feelings became mutual. His eyes spoke to her, *because* she knew them so well. An unmistakable edge of fear mixed with heavy-lidded heat and tenderness. He'd never quite looked at her like that before. The first night they'd spent together had been about lust. This was something altogether different. Softer. Sweeter. More intense. Those eyes told her he really wasn't immune to her either. They told her their exchange affected him every bit as deeply as it had her.

Panic beat behind her breastbone, even as the moment settled inside of her, a chest-crushing ache she couldn't deny, even had she wanted to. Oh, without a doubt when this weekend ended, she'd lose her heart.

He grinned suddenly, breaking the spell. His stomach muscles bunched beneath her as he lifted his head and nipped at her bottom lip. "Consider it payback."

Chapter Eight

Sebastian lay in bed, staring at the shadowy ceiling above him. After curling against his side, post-orgasmic fatigue had taken Christina. She'd fallen asleep in his arms, tucked against his side, her body warm and soft against him, her arm flung casually over his stomach. With no desire to disturb her, he'd been lying there for hours, listening to her quiet, even breathing. With no streetlights and only a few neighbors dotting the area, the house had become so silent every breath she drew and released kept him company.

He'd missed this the last night they'd spent together, but he had two hours now to luxuriate in the simple pleasure of her curves against his side. He had to admit getting to watch her sleep had a peace settling inside of him he hadn't expected. In the darkness, she was little more than a shadowy form, but the subtle floral of her perfume swirled around him, mixing with the aroma of *her* that clung to him. Noticeable only because he wasn't used to the scent. His bedroom at home smelled like him and occasionally Spike. He'd give anything for his condo to smell like her.

She made an incoherent murmur in the dark. The quiet yawn she let out next told him she'd woken. He stroked her back, unable to resist, but couldn't bring himself to pierce the beautiful silence by saying anything. She stretched against his side like a languid cat waking from a nap. Her hand slid over his stomach and up his chest, and she rolled toward him, sliding her slight weight on top of him. She didn't say a word but dipped her head and found his mouth in the darkness. She kissed him softly, a tender tangle of lips. Her body curled against him, and her hands wandered down his torso.

His libido roared to life, his cock hardening behind his fly. He slid his hands down her back, letting them wander over the soft curve of her behind. She had the most incredible skin and he luxuriated in the simple pleasure of running his hands over her, if only because he'd spent so many years wishing he could. The sensation of being a child set free in a toy store beat behind his breastbone. His heart hammered and his blood roared. For the entire weekend, this skin, this woman, was his to touch, to make love to, as he saw fit.

A twinge of pain clenched at his chest, the reminder niggling at the back of his mind. When the weekend was over, though, they were supposed go their separate ways. She'd set firm boundaries, and who could blame her? He didn't have the world's best track record. The truth was, though, holding her while she slept and the inherent intimacy it created had lodged in his chest as being so damn *right*. She belonged here, in his arms, in his life.

Christina's mouth slanted over his, her tongue pushing inside, reaching and searching. Her breath was sweet and hot. She all but purred, her body arching against him, rocking into the connection, pressing her mound into his erection. The harder she pushed, the more he ached and the louder her whimpers became.

He slid his hands down her back to her ass and cupped the supple globes in his hands, pressing her more tightly into the ridge of his erection. She groaned from down deep and shuddered. The rhythm of her rocking grew into a shaky, jerky hitch, and her body trembled against him, telling him her release was close. So he tightened his grip on her ass and rocked his hips up into her, nudging her over and over.

Her fingers curled against his body. Her nails scraped his skin through his shirt. She dropped her head into the crook of his shoulder and let out a low, agonized moan. "Oh God…"

His name rolled off her tongue on a soft cry as she shook in his arms, her hips rocking into the connection of their bodies, her breath a warm, erratic huff against his skin. When her shaking stopped, she let out a contented little *hmmm* and stretched again.

"That was delicious." She purred against his throat as she molded her mouth to the side of his neck, her lips skimming his jaw.

Desperate to be inside her, to connect to all of her this time, he reached between them, popped the button on his slacks, and slid down the zipper, freeing his cock. Then he reached into the right front pocket of his pants, pulled out the condom he'd only remembered to stash in there before coming upstairs, and held it out to her.

She took the condom from him, and, hands braced on his chest, sat upright. Her gaze burning into him, she pulled her dress up over her head and tossed it to the floor before sliding down his body. Her hot, wet folds slid along his length as she moved down enough to roll on the condom. Protection in place, she moved over him again and sank onto him in one slow stroke.

Sebastian groaned. She was hot and slippery, her body snug around him. In the darkness, he couldn't see much of anything. She became little more than a shadowy form, which made their lovemaking all the more erotic for it. He could only see shapes, the general outline of her curves rising above him, but he was hooked on what he *would* see. Her slender neck and strong shoulders. The curve of her full breasts and their slight bounce. The flare of her hips. And his cock, disappearing into her.

She rose and sank on his cock at a lazy, steady rhythm, constantly making that sound, the little purr of satisfaction that did nothing but ramp up his libido to explosive heights. Unless he was mistaken, she enjoyed herself. Christina worked his cock like she owned it, which, he had to admit, she did.

The moment sank inside of him. He couldn't deny it—he *was* all hers. The truth was, he always had been. He didn't think she knew. At least, she didn't believe him. He'd always been that guy who flitted from woman to woman, having his fill with many but settling down with none. He'd had no desire to play the fool to some woman who'd drag him around by his cock, then shatter his heart. He'd been determined never to be his father.

Christina, however, was something else. Now, more than ever, the developing closeness between them made him long to have her on a permanent basis.

He leaned over, reaching blindly for the lamp on the bedside table. His fumbling fingers hit the edge, sending it teetering. Luckily, he managed to catch it before it pitched to the floor, then settled it and found the switch. The space flooded with light. He wanted to commit every second of his time with her to memory.

Christina's eyes fluttered open. She squinted against the light before her gaze caught his. Something shifted in the small space between them. The same connection that hit him earlier pulsed again. Hands braced on his chest, she began to move over him, lifting and sinking to a slow, steady rhythm. She never once looked away and he lost himself in her beautiful green eyes. He soaked in every moment, every breath and sigh and quiet moan.

He had two days to convince her he loved her. When, exactly, he'd made the decision, he couldn't be certain. He only knew Christina was the answer to everything wrong with his life.

He sat up, wrapped his arms tightly around her, buried his face in her throat, in her scent, curling his body around hers as much as he could, and let himself go. His orgasm erupted through him in a luxurious rush. He groaned into her throat, shaking helplessly in her arms. She followed quickly on his heels. Her body trembled against him, his name leaving her lips on a litany of pleasure-filled cries that filled his soul.

When the spams ended, he buried his face in the fall of her hair, more vulnerable than he'd ever been and crushed her to him. The emotion rushed up and the words left his mouth before he could stop them. "I love you, Tina."

He waited, shaking, in silence for her to react, to say…something. Once out, he couldn't be sorry he'd said them. The words had left his mouth on a need to set them free. Where they'd take him, he didn't know. Only that he needed to say them, to give them a voice.

Christina's body stiffened, so tense her awareness of him all but crackled in the air around them. She pushed at his chest.

"Let me go." When he didn't—couldn't—release her, she shoved harder against his shoulders, struggling to free herself. "Damn it, Sebastian, let me go."

Her voice filled with panic, and he released his hold on her, forcing himself to give her some space. She scrambled off his lap as if he'd caught fire, and hightailed it out of the room without so much as a backward glance.

He flopped back onto the bed and flung an arm over his eyes. His pants lay undone. The room smelled of sex and her. He was pretty sure her sweet, feminine scent had imbedded itself in his skin, because her aroma, that luscious mix of her perfume and her own natural scent, filled his nostrils every time he inhaled, sweet and alluring.

Yet the sound of her bare feet thumping down the stairs drifted through the silence. The house and the night around them became so quiet, even the creak of a door opening drifted up the stairs.

He released a heavy breath, letting his arm flop to the bed beside him. He'd done it now. He couldn't take the words back. Truth was, he had no desire to. He might have scared the hell out of her, but he couldn't be sorry he'd said them. He wanted her. If it took him the rest of his life to earn her trust, then so be it, because he would *not* let her get away from him again.

* * *

Christina thumped down the stairs as fast as her shaky legs would carry her and strode through the living room toward the double French doors leading out to the beach. She snatched the afghan off the back of the sofa on her way through and hit the doors at a full stride, only wrapping the blanket around her naked shoulders once her bare feet hit the cool, damp wood of the back deck. Her heart pounded, and her breath lodged in her throat. She halted at the railing and drew in deep, gulping lungsful of the cool night air.

It was a beautiful night, all things considered. The sky was clear and bright, the stars twinkling above her. It was unusual to see the stars around here. The constant cloud cover always hid them, and they reflected on the surface of the water, diamonds in a midnight sky. The water lapped at the shore, quiet and serene, but the calm dark water and the beauty of her surroundings did nothing to soothe her frazzled nerves. Not this time.

Her mind reeled, going in a thousand directions at once. Sebastian's words repeated in her head. *"I love you, Tina."* Every time they replayed, her heart clenched a little harder and the tears she tried desperately to hold in pricked at the backs of her eyelids.

Memories flitted through her mind faster than she could stop them. A cruel man's idea of a game. She'd played the part of the fool for Craig. They'd dated for a year. He wooed her, made her fall in love with him, asked her to marry him and convinced her to elope. Stupid, hopeful fool that she was, she fell for his lies hook, line, and sinker. A silly girl with a romantic dream. The lonely ache had gotten to her. The desperate need for someone to see *her.*

She'd left that Las Vegas wedding chapel feeling like a damn fool. That was the day she'd realized in stunning clarity what her future would look like. Lonely and empty. Love apparently wasn't meant for her and men appeared to only see her as a means to line their pockets or their beds or any combination of both. She'd decided that night to stop trying, to dive into taking her company straight to the top.

Sebastian made her want it. She longed to believe his sweet words, but was he even capable of giving her all of himself?

Another memory lodged in her mind's eye. A heart-to-heart conversation between women. Jean had confided in her, two years ago now, after she'd ended her relationship with him. Even now the pain in the other woman's voice rose as sharp as it had then.

The door leading onto the deck creaked open behind her and Christina straightened her shoulders, trying to prepare herself for the confrontation to come. She was a businesswoman, damn it. If she could deal with men in the boardroom, Sebastian ought to be a cakewalk.

Except as she whirled to face him, the sight of him took her by surprise. Having taken off his shirt, he leaned against the doorway, arms folded, eyes hooded. His bare chest tormented her with the memory of falling asleep in his arms. Stray strands of his hair stuck out from his head, as if someone had run their fingers through it, which she knew damn well someone had. Those were *her* finger tracks in his hair. He looked exactly what he was, well and thoroughly fucked, and God, he looked sexy in it. That she wasn't still wrapped in his arms and drifting back to sleep made her chest ache.

She straightened her shoulders and pointed a finger at him, determined to regain her equilibrium. "Don't. Don't toy with me, Sebastian. I'm not one of those flighty little floozies who eat up anything you tell them."

He didn't say anything in return but pushed away from the doorway and crossed the deck, coming to a stop in front of her. She clutched the blanket tighter around her, the only defense she had against him. Nobody made her as vulnerable as he did. With all her cards laid out on the table, he had the power to break her.

Sebastian, however, didn't appear to be listening. He

backed her against the railing and pressed his long, lean body into hers.

"You think too damn much, Christina." He slid his hand into her hair and pulled her mouth to his.

A surprised gasp escaped her, but any form of protest she might have had became lost in his assault. Sebastian didn't have a timid bone in his body. He kissed the same way, bold and possessive. He wrapped his body around her, until there wasn't an inch of her not surrounded in him. His lips moved over hers like a hot brand. His tongue thrust into her mouth, searching out hers, and God help her, she reciprocated. The sensual slide of their tongues tangling had her forgetting her name.

When her head fell back on a helpless sigh—because what woman in her right mind could defend herself against Sebastian Blake in seduction mode?—he finally released her.

Now at his mercy, all she could do was shake her head. "What are you doing, Baz?"

"Not giving up on you." Even in the moonlight, the heat in his eyes scorched her. His chest rose and fell at a rapid pace with his harsh, erratic breathing.

He didn't wait for a reply but bent and swept her off her feet, afghan and all, and headed back into the house. Inside, he set her on the sofa, then leaned over her, hands planted on either side of her, and pressed a soft kiss to her mouth. Lips a hairsbreadth away, his gaze filled with a heat and determination that liquefied her insides and made her breath catch. This was Sebastian, the deter-mined CEO and seductive playboy. The man knew how to sweep a woman off her feet, and he knew *her* too well.

"I'm going to light a fire. Don't. Move." Despite his all-business tone, his finger traced the shell of her ear and down her cheek to the edge of her jaw. "If you run again, I *will* chase you, and when I catch you, I'll throw you over my knees and redden your ass."

His words had goose bumps popping up along her skin. A heated tremor ran the length of her spine. The idea of him reddening her bottom had a wave of heat zinging straight into her core, and her clit throbbed in eager anticipation of the pleasure that would surely follow. Oh, she loved a good spanking during sex. She was half tempted to run, if only to see if he'd make good on his threat. They had explosive passion together, and the sex that followed would no doubt blow her mind.

Not that she had any intention of giving in so easily.

She sat straighter and narrowed her eyes at him. "You wouldn't dare."

He nipped at her bottom lip, hard enough to sting, then soothed the bite with a flick of his tongue before pulling back enough to meet her gaze. "Try me, baby."

He rose to his feet, strode to the stone fireplace, and squatted. He set about stacking wood onto the metal grate and wadding bits of newspaper. Every inch of her trembled. In anticipation. In fear. Up until this weekend, Sebastian had never aimed that seductive prowess in her direction. He'd never looked at her with so much determined heat. He'd never spoken to her that way, either. He'd surprised her at the auction, and he did so again now. Shivers chased each other over the surface of her skin even as dread sank in the pit of her stomach. Every cell in her body sat poised, waiting for him to make his next move. How the hell was she supposed to keep her distance from him when he insisted on breaching every wall she had?

When the kindling finally flared to life, Sebastian added a piece of wood, sat back on his heels, elbow braced on his knees, and stared into the flames. After several moments, he sank onto his bottom on the pile of blankets laid out in front of the fire. When and how he'd gathered them, she had no idea, but he'd created a cozy little spot in front of the fireplace. A bunch of pillows and blankets all piled on the thick rug. He leaned back against the end of the recliner situated catty-corner to the fireplace, the flickering light dancing over his features, and crooked a finger at her.

God help her. She couldn't say no. Her feet moved of their own accord, pulling her to him like mice after the pied piper.

"Sit." He held out his hand in invitation, and the gleam in his eye dared her to deny him.

Unable to, she slipped her hand into his and did as he bade, positioning herself between his thighs. Sebastian settled her back against his chest and wrapped his arms around her. Only by sheer force of will did she manage to bite back the contented sigh that wanted to escape her. His embrace gave her the sensation of having come home.

For a few moments, only the fire's crackles and pops disrupted the silence. The orange and yellow flames chased away the chill and illuminated the otherwise darkened room with a warm glow. It might have been beautiful had her stomach not been tied in a thousand knots.

"Want to tell me about him?"

His quiet voice rumbled against her back, his warm breath teasing her right ear. The question had her stiffening, anxiousness tightening her stomach. He knew something, or at least had figured something out. Right then, she felt naked and vulnerable, like all her secrets were laid bare before him. "Tell you about who?"

His arms tightened around her, drawing her farther back into him. "Whoever it was you were thinking of when you ran from the room. The asshat who doesn't deserve the penance you're giving him. Was it Alan?"

Alan. The self-serving jerk she'd dated before she met Craig. Sebastian had hated him. Then again, Sebastian hadn't liked any of her boyfriends.

Christina released a heavy breath and relented. She'd promised him honesty, and because the lure to share her heart, however foolish, was too strong to deny. "No, Craig."

He let out an irritated growl, his body stiffening behind her. "I always hated him. Arrogant son of a bitch. What'd he do?"

The urge to tell him, to lean her head back on his shoulder, rose strong within her. The protectiveness in his tone, in his body language, melted every last defense she had. As much as they butted heads, he'd always looked out for her. It was why she'd fallen in love with him in the first place.

"You never liked any of the guys I dated." She closed her eyes. Her heart thudded a dull beat in her veins, the ache already blossoming. How she ever thought she could spend this time with him and not fall deeper in love with him she didn't know.

"Because I was jealous, but most of them never deserved you. They never treated you right." He leaned his chin on her shoulder, pressing his cheek to hers. "Tell me."

His stubble pricked her skin. His scent enveloped her, mixing with the earthy smell of the wood smoke. The lull in his voice, his solid warmth, and his arms around her coaxed the words from her lips. With a sigh of surrender, she dropped her head back on his shoulder. "We went down to Vegas. Do you remember?"

"Mmm. You came back early. That was the weekend you broke up. What happened? He give in to the call of the strippers?" He leaned back, relaxing into the chair behind him, taking her with him. His hands settled in her lap, his thumbs stroking her bare belly in an idle fashion.

His touch made her body hum, but the conversation pulled up memories she wanted to forget. She laughed, harsh and bitter, as they played through her mind. "Of all things for you to ask, Baz."

His body tensed against her back. His keen awareness of her right then sparked in the air. "He did, didn't he?"

The irritated bite in his tone had her stomach twisting. She'd always assumed his overprotectiveness of her to be a big brother thing. After all, Caden had done the same from time to time, not so subtly letting a date know he was watching. Now, given Sebastian's vulnerable confession upstairs, she wondered. Had she ever really seen him at all? Was their entire relationship based on misconceptions and half-truths? She loathed telling him the truth now.

She bit her lower lip. She'd never told anyone this, Caden included. She'd been too embarrassed to admit she'd fallen for such blatant lies. She'd followed her heart and let down her guard.

"Yes. We went down there to get married." She closed her eyes and swallowed hard. An embarrassed heat rose up her neck and into her cheeks. She'd been such a fool. "We were supposed to meet at one of the chapels, but when he got there, another woman threw herself into his arms. Turned out, she was waiting for him, too."

Sebastian went eerily still. Tension filled the surrounding air, yet he remained silent. So silent his thoughts all but screamed at her. Her hands trembled. Dread and melancholy sank in her stomach and every cell in her body waited for his reaction, as if poised on a cliff, seconds away from being shoved over the edge.

Finally, she couldn't stand it. "Baz, say something."

"What do you want me to say? I'm thrilled? I need to get up." Irritation rose in his voice. He didn't wait for her response but released his hold on her and stood. He didn't so much as blink in her direction before he stepped around her and stalked from the room, strides long and determined as he yanked the back door open and strode out onto the deck.

As she righted herself, hurt pinged around in her chest like a rubber bouncy ball in a small room. Gut instinct told her to leave the moment where it was. After all, distance between them was better than the closeness. His sudden anger, though, left her bereft and confused. She'd confided in him, and he responded like that? Damn it. She had to know why, and whether she liked the answer or not, he was going to tell her.

Despite her better judgment, she rose and followed, stopping in the doorway. "When I was angry with you earlier, you wouldn't let me run and hide. You followed me and insisted I sit with you and tell you. If you're pissed at me, you owe it to me to talk to me."

"All right." Sebastian whirled to face her. A wild mixture of vulnerability, frustration, and raw pain shined in his eyes. "You want to know? I'll tell you. How the hell could you want to marry *him*, but I get the door slammed in my face?"

The emotion in his eyes had her halting in her tracks, her bare feet gluing to the damp boards beneath her. She hadn't expected him to say that. She'd expected...she didn't even know, but not that. Clearly she'd hurt him. Her immediate denial when they'd arrived had apparently hit its intended target—to set him in his place. Suddenly, she wasn't so proud of always being the strong one, because the pain in his eyes wrenched at her heart.

She stepped toward him, shook her head. "I was a different person back then, Sebastian. In a lot of ways, what Craig did changed the way I dealt with relationships. As for you? You were never an option. You were always just the unobtainable fantasy."

He stared for a beat before turning to the railing and stood looking out toward the waters of the lake. "Mmm.

And I'm entirely too aware that I'm exactly like him, because it's what I've always shown you."

His voice came as quiet as the night, barely a murmur above the cool breeze blowing around them. After a moment, he finally looked back. He stared again, eyes reaching and searching. Apparently having made whatever decision he'd been pondering, he closed the distance between them, caught her around the waist, and pulled her against him.

"You said you wanted honesty, but I'm not sure you're ready to hear it. I was lying in bed holding you tonight, staring at the ceiling, realizing you fit. In my arms. In my life. I realized you always have. Nobody has ever taken care of me the way you do. At least, nobody who wasn't paid to do it. My mother left me when I was ten, dumped me like yesterday's trash. My father treated me like I was his greatest disappointment. But you?"

He shook his head and lifted a finger, stroking the side of her face. An odd mixture of emotion played in his eyes. Awe. Confusion. The tenderness staring back at her stole the breath from her lungs. More sides of Sebastian he'd never shown her until recently, and she became caught, hooked on his tender words.

"Even when I'm an asshole, you still come to me on my worst day and hold me while I sleep. I'm terrified of losing you, Tina. You want to know why I always pushed you away? That's it."

He turned his head, buried his face in her throat, and skimmed his mouth up her neck and across her jaw. Everywhere he kissed had shivers chasing each other over the surface of her skin. Her breathing hitched. Her bones melted, muscles loosening, sagging into the warmth of his body, into his tender touch. Because he *did* have one.

God, she'd never expected Sebastian to be such a tender lover. He didn't fuck her to sate a need. He made love to her. Oh, she'd been with enough men over the years to know the difference. Sebastian stroked her body, took pleasure in her pleasure. Even when sex was fast and hard, because too many years of denial had broken down the dam, he still held her a little too tightly; his gaze still penetrated hers. Like he could see right into her soul and gave his own in return.

Now his heart-filled words, the vulnerability in his voice…How did she fight that?

"But I can't do it anymore. I can't pretend you mean nothing to me. I can't make love to you all weekend and then let you go. I can't go back to seeing you date those assholes or watch another loser like Craig break your heart and pretend I don't want to rip his fucking head off." His body tensed, his voice taking on an irritated edge, but as quickly as the anger came, he drew a breath and released it. "I can't have another meaningless fling and pretend it's what I want, either."

"Isn't it?" She closed her eyes, trying to regain her equilibrium. It wasn't fair for him to tell her these things. She knew him. At some point, he'd get scared and he'd run. They all did. "Jean was in love with you, you know. She confided in me once, after you broke up."

She'd wanted to hate Jean for getting what she'd coveted, but she couldn't. Several weeks after their relationship ended, she'd run across Jean and could only feel sorry for her.

Christina knew only too well what it meant to love Sebastian.

His shoulders slumped. "I know. She told me. I hated myself for having to let her down, but I had to be honest with her. I was honest with her from the start. She knew going in I wouldn't. I never lied to her or promised her more. At the time, getting married meant a death sentence for me. Damned if I'd become my father.

"Now, after having made love to you, the thought of going back to the way we were makes my gut ache. I'll never be able to go back to those meaningless flings. This time with you has changed me." His voice lowered to a vulnerable murmur. He pressed his cheek to hers, his breath warm in her ear. "I'm safe with you. That's what you do for me, Tina. For the first time in my life, I'm safe with someone."

He straightened, then took a step back, swept her off her feet, and strode into the house. She opened her mouth to protest, but he shook his head, silencing the words before they could leave her tongue.

"I'm done talking. You want to know how I feel about you? I'm going to spend the next two days showing you."

He carried her back into the house and set her down on the pile of pillows and blankets he'd set out on the rug earlier. He crawled between her thighs, forcing her to lie back, and settled his body over hers.

Holding himself on his elbows, he bent his head, his voice a husky murmur as his soft lips caressed the skin of her throat. His teeth scraped the curve of her jaw. His tongue flicked out to taste her, singeing the all too sensitive skin behind her earlobe. "If you can walk Sunday, you're free to run, but this weekend, baby, you're mine."

He didn't give her time to speak or to think, let alone protest. His hands roamed her body, stroking and caressing with the lightest of touches. So gently, he lit every inch of her on fire. All the while his mouth was everywhere and his hips rocked gently against hers, nudging the tip of his erection, still hidden behind his zipper, against her sweet spot.

Sebastian, apparently, had every intention of proving he owned her. In minutes, he had her a trembling mess. Every inch of her had come alive with a desperate, unslakable desire. For him. Only for him. No man's touch had ever been so good or so right, and any thought of leaving fled, lost in him.

Holding himself on one elbow, Sebastian reached between them, undid his fly, and pushed into her in one powerful thrust. She didn't have to ask to know he was staking his claim, and her body vibrated with the power of it.

Christina gasped, the bliss engulfing her. She wrapped her arms and legs around him, holding him to her. She could deny it all she wanted, but she needed him. She needed *this*.

Because she loved him.

Oh, she'd thought she'd loved him before, but it felt like child's play, a schoolgirl's crush, compared to this. Nothing had prepared her for finding a connection between them.

God help her. When Sunday morning came, she had a tough decision to make. Would he ever really be able to give her all of himself? He hadn't been able to for Jean. Jean had spent three years of her life with him. Deep down, Sebastian was a good man, and Jean had waited, hoping. But in the end, he'd let her go, because she wanted more than he could give her. Her pain that day in the coffee shop had been palpable, the look on her face forever etched in Christina's mind.

What if, three years from now, that was her? Was she really ready to do it again? To pin her hopes on something that may end exactly the same way it had ended for poor Jean?

She didn't know. She'd promised him the weekend, though. If she expected him to keep his end of the bargain, she had to give him the same. This weekend, she'd allow his sweet words to fill her with hope. She'd decide when the weekend was over.

Chapter Nine

Christina set her pen on the kitchen counter and lifted her gaze, peering out the French doors across the room. It was early Sunday morning. The sun had begun to rise above the horizon, streaking the sky outside with oranges and yellows. The peek of blue and distinct lack of gray in the skyline held the promise of a gorgeous day, though weather reports had told her it wouldn't stay that way.

She folded the letter neatly, picked up her heels from the floor, hooked them with her left hand, and moved into the living room. The fire they'd built the night before had long since burned itself out. Sebastian lay sound asleep on the makeshift bed he'd built Friday night, covered from the waist down by a handmade quilt. One hand lay on his bare chest, the other flung over his eyes. His chest rose and fell at a steady pace. He looked peaceful and oddly beautiful.

Melancholy clenched at her chest. She'd spent the weekend making love to him. In between, they'd spent hours talking. They'd taken long walks around the lake and had a picnic in her father's boat out in the middle of the cool water. For the last two days, she'd allowed herself to get lost in him, in the promise in his eyes. Because she'd promised him she would. And because she needed to know for herself.

Outside, the popping of rocks beneath tires drifted through the silence. Her cell buzzed in her hand a few seconds later, and a quick glance confirmed her limo had arrived. Her gaze returned to Sebastian. The idea of leaving him this way had a cold ache forming in her chest. He'd wake alone. It would be the second time she'd snuck out while he slept. Oh, for sure he'd be angry when he woke, but this was an argument she couldn't have with him. At least not now. Her emotions were all on the surface this morning. Waking to him, after having spent the last two nights making love to him, had left her emotions a giant tangled web in her chest.

He was right. He fit. Like Cinderella's lost glass slipper. Or a worn favorite pair of jeans. No matter how many times you washed them or how many holes they got, they still had the perfect fit and they still felt like home. She didn't think it possible to love him more than she already did, but he'd proved her wrong. She hadn't counted on there being a connection between them.

Which was exactly why she had to leave. She had a big decision to make. She knew now that Sebastian had told her nothing but the truth this weekend. That he cared was in everything he did. The way he touched her. The tenderness in his eyes when he looked at her. All those sweet gifts he'd sent after the first night they'd spent together. The coffee, the lunches, the cookies. Clearly, she'd had him pegged all wrong.

But her questions remained. Could he really be what she needed? Could he really devote himself to her and only her? Did it even matter anymore?

She'd never figure it out here with him. Here, they were in an intimate little cocoon where the entire rest of the world didn't exist. If she stayed, if they took the ride home together, Sebastian would no doubt attempt to persuade her to his side. With his addicting kisses and wandering hands and his heartfelt admissions.

When what they needed was time. She needed time. To figure herself out. What she wanted, from him and from this relationship. What she was willing to risk for it. Deep down, *did* she really trust him? Was she willing to risk her heart, knowing it could all end the same way it had for poor Jean?

Only time would tell her that.

No, as cruel as it was to leave him this way, she'd only promised him the weekend, and it was over.

She crossed the space and leaned the note she'd written against the stone hearth, then knelt beside him. She kissed his forehead, then pushed to her feet and forced herself to turn and walk away. She closed the front door quietly behind her.

* * *

Several hours later, Christina sat in her tiny kitchen, staring absently out the window across the room. The large picture window was half the reason she'd bought this house. It gave her a spectacular view of the line of trees out in her backyard, swaying in the gentle breeze. The day had turned out glorious. Blue skies, puffy white clouds. They even had actual sun. The golden gleam filled her kitchen, illuminating the space.

Her fingers curled around her coffee cup, but the liquid within had long since gone cold. The muffin she'd warmed up sat untouched on the small china plate. Even though she hadn't eaten in over twelve hours, she wasn't hungry. She couldn't stop thinking about Sebastian. The image of him, asleep on their makeshift bed, had burned itself into her mind. It replayed now like a CD with a scratch, taunting her. So did the thought of him waking alone and finding her gone. Was he angry? Hurt? The idea alone was a wound on her heart.

Coming home, she'd thought it would take her days to figure herself out, what she wanted. Was she willing to risk her heart again, knowing it could end the same way? Sitting here now, the overwhelming truth slid over her. She didn't have to think and she didn't need time. She knew what she wanted.

Him. She missed him. The thought of never again getting to experience what they had this weekend left her with an emptiness inside.

It made no sense, really. Logic told her they needed to take it slow, reminded her that she'd sworn after Craig she'd never rush headlong into a serious relationship. Neither could she deny the truth staring her in the face. Her mind kept going round and round a single point: whether it lasted one year or forever, she still wanted him.

This weekend had only proven one thing—that if anybody was worth taking a chance on, it was him. It had been in his touch. He'd staked his claim on her and every cell in her body said she was his. From the tip of her nose to the roots of her hair to the soles of her feet. Every molecule belonged to him.

The buzz of the front doorbell sounded through the house, interrupting her thoughts. With a sigh, she abandoned her cold breakfast and made her way to the foyer. She forced a polite smile but it fell the instant she pulled open the door. On the other side of the threshold, Sebastian stood with his arms folded across his chest, an angry scowl forming deep grooves between his brows. A five o'clock shadow graced his jaw, suggesting he hadn't been home yet.

Her heart hammered. Cleary he'd come straight here. Though why she should have expected anything less, she didn't know. Sebastian wasn't the type of man who took no for an answer. He faced problems head-on and worked at them until he found a clear answer. He'd always teased her for the way she barged into his life, but the truth was, he did it, too. They really were alike in that respect.

"You have this really bad habit of running out while I'm asleep."

Her heartbeat picked up speed, sending her blood racing through her veins. She swallowed hard. He'd come to confront her. She dropped her gaze to the floor, flexing her toes against the dark wood. Heat flooded her cheeks and the right words refused to come.

She closed her eyes for a moment and drew a lungful of much needed oxygen, drawing in courage along with it. He deserved the truth.

A little more settled, she opened her eyes again and forced herself to meet his gaze. "I'm scared, Sebastian. After Craig, I promised myself I'd never do it again, I'd never be someone's naïve fool, following my heart."

He dropped his arms and crossed the threshold, stepped into her personal space, and backed her against the wall adjacent to the doorway. He set his hands on either side of her head. The look on his face, a mixture of tenderness and heat and a touch of irritation, had her breath halting in her lungs. "I know. And I know you said you needed time, but I came over to warn you. I've made a decision I'm setting into motion this morning. I'm also here to tell you that if you think I'm going to let you walk out of my life and go back to the nothing we had, you need to think again."

Christina opened her mouth and shook her head, ready to explain, but Sebastian pinched her lips shut. When she mumbled a protest, he grinned, white-toothed and sexy as hell. When she quieted, he released her mouth.

"No more arguments. Do what you have to do. Run. Keep me at arm's length. I don't care. I'll wait. You're right. I hurt Jean. The truth is, I had to let her go because I didn't love her the way she loved me." He leaned in again, this time so close his warm, minty breath whispered over her lips. "So, you do what you have to do, baby, but mark my words. One day, Christina McKenzie, I *will* marry you. I'll wait you out for as long as I have to, but you should know me well enough by now to know I don't give up easily."

He brushed his mouth over hers, the softest of kisses, enough to melt her knees, then stepped back.

"We'll talk more later. I've made an appointment with my lawyer."

And with that, he disappeared out the door. By the time she'd managed to calm her breathing and find her brain again, the quiet purr of his limo's engine was fading into the distance.

As she straightened off the wall, his words came back to her. *"I came over to warn you. I've made a decision I'm setting in motion this morning."*

Her mind flitted through a million possibilities, then settled on one with heart-stopping clarity. His father's will. She bit her lower lip, gnashing it between her teeth. But what did he mean? Set *what* into motion?

Determination swelled behind her like a locomotive. She didn't know, but she knew who might. Caden.

She strode into the kitchen, grabbed her purse off the table, slipped on some heels, and jogged out the door to her car in the driveway. She'd coax the truth out of Caden if she had to.

Five minutes later, she stepped out of the elevator into the private vestibule of Caden and Hannah's condo downtown. She knocked on the door, then stepped back to wait. Silence came from within. Being a Saturday, she shouldn't be surprised, but Caden had always been a morning person.

She knocked again. This time distinct grumbling registered on the other side and the door finally opened. Caden's tall, broad form filled the doorway.

Wearing only his pajama bottoms and an irritated scowl, he folded his arms. "Do I look like Grand Central Station to you? Can't you people sleep in on Sunday?"

"Oh, let her in." Hannah's soft voice drifted from behind him. Seconds later, the door pulled open wider and Hannah appeared at his side, wearing a pale pink satin robe. She offered a gentle smile and leaned forward to wrap Christina in a hug. Hannah released her and gripped her hand instead, squeezing it. "Ignore Grumpy here. He hasn't had his coffee yet."

Caden's scowl deepened. "It isn't the coffee I'm missing right now."

Hannah jerked her gaze to his, flushing to the roots of her hair. Clearly she'd interrupted more than breakfast.

"Oh my." Her cheeks heating, Christina flashed an apologetic frown. "I'm so sorry to…interrupt. Baz came over this morning. Caden, he told me he's setting something into motion—that he's going to see his lawyer. What did he mean? And, please, don't pretend you don't know. You two have been joined at the hip since first grade. I know darn well he likely called you first."

He sighed, dropped his arms, and stepped back, ushering her inside with a sweep of his hand. She followed him over the threshold and closed the door behind her.

Hannah flashed a polite smile, her eyes bright and warm. "Would you like some coffee?"

Christina shook her head. "No, thank you. I'm so sorry to impose. I won't stay long, I promise."

Hannah pursed her lips and waved a dismissive hand. "Sweetie, don't even mention it. We weren't sleeping, and I need to feed this little guy anyway." She rubbed her belly, her eyes taking on a loving, tender glow. She turned to Caden. "I'll go make some coffee and give you two time to talk."

"Thanks, babe." He wrapped an arm around Hannah's back, pulled her in for a tender, lingering kiss, and waited until she waddled off toward the back of the house before turning to Christina. His earlier scowl returned. "He called me an hour ago. He's officially refusing his father's demands and signing the company over to the wife."

Shock moved through her system, and for a moment, she could only stare, heart hammering in her ears. As Caden's news settled in, a mixture of pain and regret clenched at her chest. Oh God. Had she forced him to make a difficult decision, to choose between her and his work?

She shook her head in misery, his form blurring before her as her gaze unfocused. "Because I told him I wouldn't marry him."

"I'll let him fill you in. It's his story." Caden lifted a brow. "Care to tell me what happened? It kind of surprised me to hear from him this morning. He sounded hell-bent. Now suddenly here you are. What on earth happened?"

She nodded absently and dropped her gaze to the floor, studying the lines in the dark polished wood. From somewhere further inside, the sounds of water running filled the unbearable silence.

"I told him at the start of the weekend I wouldn't marry him, and I left the cabin early this morning before he woke. Which is probably why he came to you first thing." She looked up, meeting his gaze. "I'm scared, Caden. I wasn't sure if I could really trust that he could be what I thought I needed, but this morning I was sitting at home alone, and I realized it didn't matter. I still want him. That's crazy, right?"

He sighed, took her by the shoulders, and drew her to him, enveloping her in his strong embrace. "Do you recall what you said to me when I stood onstage at the auction last year, after Hannah walked out?"

Christina laid her head on his chest, allowing herself the luxury of accepting the comfort he offered. They'd always been close. Whatever went on between them, no matter how angry they got at each other, Caden was always there, and not for the first time, she was grateful for his strength and support.

Her mind filled with the exact memory he mentioned. Christina didn't have to ask to understand where this conversation was headed.

"I asked you if you loved her." She'd never forget the panic in his eyes when Hannah left the room. She'd known right then he'd found his other half, because out of all the women who'd crossed his life, she'd never seen that look on his face before.

"And?"

A shudder of misery ran through her as her heart shouted the answer to his unspoken question.

"I love him. Desperately. The thought of going back to

what we were, the nothing…" Her forehead rocked against his chest. "I can't pretend nothing happened between us or go back to being nothing more to him than your sister. Now you tell me he's signing the resorts over to his stepmother? I can't let him do that, especially if he's doing it for me."

"I don't think he's doing it for entirely you, but…" He let out a sigh. "Yeah. That's exactly how I felt, too, when Hannah walked out of the auction. I panicked. Wondered if I'd ever see her again. Do you remember your advice to me that night?"

Though she had a sneaking suspicion why he was asking, she looked up, needing to see his eyes. "I told you to go after her."

"I'm giving you the same advice." He pressed a kiss to her forehead and his voice lowered to a gentle murmur. "Go get him. He's in love with you, too. I've known for a long time. You're right. He doesn't have the best track record, but even I know he'd give his life for you. Even if he is too stubborn to admit it."

"He did. Admit it, I mean." Her heart clenched with the memory. The vulnerability in Sebastian's voice when he whispered the words made her ache all over again. He'd meant them. Those words from his mouth had scared the hell out of her.

"Ah. Now we're getting somewhere. He spooked you."

She couldn't deny the truth of his statement. Sebastian had done exactly that, in large part because she hadn't expected him to. She was so afraid he'd be another Craig, so sure of the image she'd always had of him.

Caden's arms tightened around her for a brief moment; then he pulled back, holding her by the upper arms. His gaze had softened, now filling with gentle understanding. Growing up, he'd been her best friend, and over the years, they'd fought, as siblings often do, but when she needed him, Caden was always there. Even if he was so ticked at her he didn't want to speak to her, she could always count on him when she needed him most. He was a standup guy, and it made him an excellent husband. She'd always known it would.

"Go after him. If you love him, too, Chris, you have to take the chance. There's nobody better for you or more worth taking a chance on than him. And I'm not saying that because he's my best friend. He'd do anything for you, and all he really wants is for you to be happy. It's all he's ever wanted." Caden pressed another kiss to her forehead, then released her, pulled the front door open, and nodded in the direction of the quiet vestibule beyond. "Go. You'll regret it if you don't."

* * *

Sebastian paced from one end of the living room to the other and back again. The city below him hummed with early morning activity as it slowly came awake. The harbor out beyond was calm and beautiful, but he couldn't relax. He gave Lupe the weekends off, and the condo was too damn quiet.

An hour had passed since he'd left Christina standing in

her foyer. His visit to his lawyer had been successful. The deal was done. Yet his stomach was still tied into a mass of nervous, tense knots. There was still one loose end. Christina. He'd woken this morning alone in front of a cold fireplace. The lack of her warmth against his side and the eerie quiet of the house had seeped over him. He didn't need her note to know she'd snuck out while he slept.

He'd laid on those blankets, staring at the ceiling, for over an hour. Yeah, discovering she'd left him again without so much as a goodbye had hurt, and his heart had sank into his toes. He'd gone over everything he'd said to her the night before and everything he wanted to say to her as soon as he found her. He'd gone through about every emotion as well, from betrayal to anger to remorse. In the end, only one thing mattered.

Her. In the span of five minutes, as he finally picked himself up off the floor, got dressed, and called his driver to come get him, the decision only solidified in his mind. He'd been her, scared and running. He'd spent most of their adult lives running from the way he felt about her. He couldn't give up on her now. He needed her too much. If it meant he had to wait for her to become comfortable with the changes in their relationship, then he'd wait. If he gave up on her, then he didn't deserve her, because she'd never given up on him.

He had to admit it felt good to take his life back, to spit his father's last dying demand back in his face. He'd have to spend millions investing in a company that should have been his by default. Not to mention he was only making his stepmother richer, but he didn't care. The hotels and resorts would finally be his. With any luck, so would Christina.

The doorbell sounded through the house, and Spike, seated in his usual spot on the windowsill, hopped down and took off running for the door.

Sebastian followed with less enthusiasm. "I doubt it's her, buddy."

He wished, but it was likely too soon to hope for much from Christina. He'd have to take his time with her and prove he meant what he said. She was it for him, the one and only, and if he had to wait another twenty years for her to marry him, then so be it.

He paused at the door, drew a deep breath, and ran a hand over his face. He had to admit, he wasn't up for visitors. He had to look haggard at best. He hadn't even shaved, hadn't showered. All he'd really done was change his clothes and brush his teeth.

Pulling open the door, though, he found exactly what he hadn't expected. Christina. She stood wearing a white blouse and a gray pencil skirt that ended at her knees. Her hair fell to her shoulders in soft waves. She looked beautiful as always.

He barely registered the tears in her eyes before she launched herself at him. She threw her arms around his neck and plastered her mouth to his. Too surprised and too damn grateful to see her to do much more than react, his arms closed around her of their own accord. Her soft mouth slanted over his and joy and relief expanded in his chest. He crushed her to him and kissed her back with everything he had. He didn't care why she'd come or why the hell she was kissing him. Only that she was.

Barely a couple of hours had passed since he'd last held her, but God, he'd missed her. Missed the simple joy of kissing her because he had the need, and her mouth was heaven. Soft, warm, and inviting, her lips played over his with quiet desperation and her body molded to his. That she'd come had to be a good sign, and he latched on to the small measure of hope like a fallen log in turbulent water.

When he was lost and crumbling at her feet, she pulled back. Her brow furrowed, fierce determination rising in her eyes. "It's my turn now."

He let out a quiet laugh and stroked a hand down her cheek. That was Christina in a nutshell, bossy and strong-willed, but doing it all with her heart on her sleeve. God how he loved her for it. "Yes, ma'am."

She released a breath, and her entire demeanor softened. Her eyes raked over his face, searching with apprehension and worry. "I can't let you do this."

He released a heavy breath, forced himself to let her go, and stepped back. If he didn't, he'd be pushing her up against the nearest wall and kissing her until she relented. He had to take this at her pace, whatever that meant. "You've obviously spoken with Cade. I'm sorry, but this isn't your decision. I'm taking my life back. I refuse to cave to my father's demands again. There's only one woman I want to marry."

She stepped forward, following him, refusing to let him run and hide, as usual, and laid a hand on his chest. "I won't let you give up your life's work for me."

He shook his head. "I appreciate that. I really do. But finding you gone reaffirmed something for me. You're my future, Tina. My heart and everything I've ever wanted. I think you always have been. Just took me a while to come to terms with it. What did you tell me? That if you were ever going to marry me, it had to be because I loved you, because I couldn't live without you? Well, I can't." He picked up her hand and stroked his thumb over the backs of her knuckles. "I want forever. Not a year or to satisfy my father's selfish demands."

He lifted her fingers to his mouth and brushed a kiss across her knuckles, then forced himself to step back and tucked his hands in his pockets. The need to pull her back rose too strongly and this decision had to be hers and hers alone. He needed her to come to him this time.

"I'm waiting until the time limit runs out so that *when* you marry me, I don't want there to be any doubt in your mind I'm doing it because the thought of living the rest of my life without you by my side and in my arms makes my gut ache." He winked at her. "Notice I said *when*, not *if.* I'll wait for you as long as I have to."

Her shoulders slumped and tears flooded her eyes, sparkling in the sunlight flooding through the condo. Her voice wobbled as she spoke. "I'm sorry I left. Like I said in my note, I just wanted time. Waking up beside you felt so damn right. I wanted it, Baz. I wanted to wake up beside you every morning and fall asleep in your arms every night, and—"

"Why are you here, Tina?" It was a dumb question given the way she'd kissed him, but he needed to hear her actually say the words.

"To stop you from giving up the resorts. And to tell you I love you." Her tears broke free, several leaking down her cheeks, her eyes filling with a gut-wrenching misery. "I was scared. I was terrified I'd be another Jean to you, and—"

Relief shuddered through him, a joy so keen he would have shouted had he not been so damn stunned. She hadn't come to stop him from giving up his company. She'd come because she couldn't live without him either.

He slid a hand into her hair, pulled her to him, and settled his mouth over hers, silencing the rest of whatever the hell she'd planned to say. That was all he needed to hear. The rest was unimportant. Only that she'd come because she wanted *him.*

With a quiet, maddening whimper, her body melted into him, and he lost himself in the sweetness of her mouth. He groaned and settled his arms around her, crushing her to him and took everything she gave. He'd never been happier to see anyone in his life. He was so goddamn lucky to have her.

When they finally parted, both were breathless. Her gaze filled with tenderness, with the newness of the moment. With the same relief shuddering through him. Her fingers clutched his back, holding him every bit as tight, and his future shined in her gorgeous eyes. Only now did he realize it always had. He'd do whatever it took not to lose her.

"Marry me, Tina." The words left his mouth before he'd even had a chance to ponder *how* he wanted to ask her, but he wasn't sorry he'd said them.

She gave him a watery smile and stroked her palm down his cheek. "I thought you'd never ask."

He settled his hands around her waist, unwilling to let her go yet. "I meant what I said, though. I won't marry you until after the three months are over."

Worry creased her brow. "Baz, you can't give up."

He flashed a grin. "When have you ever known me to give up? My father's will states if I don't comply, the company reverts to Gwen, though I get to stay on as CEO. Since it's a sole proprietorship, technically, once it's hers, she's free to do whatever she wants with it. She can sell it if she wants. The incorporation documents set up when my father founded the company years ago said pretty much the same thing."

Christina's stiff posture deflated, and she wrapped her arms around him, hugging him tightly. "I still think you shouldn't give up. It's sweet, Baz, but it's not necessary. I'd marry you *now*."

"This part at least had very little to do with you. You were more motivation to get the ball rolling this morning. I won't give my father the satisfaction of knowing he bent me to his will even from beyond the fucking grave." He tightened his arms around her, holding her close, enjoying the simple feel of her. The tension between them now gone, relief shuddered through him. She'd come back to him. "I called Gwen on the way to your place, right after I called Cade. I have to admit she surprised the hell out of me. She agreed to sell me the company. She says she doesn't want it, and she never wanted to make trouble with me. She said she wasn't *in* love with my father, but she did love him. Said he was kind to her, and all she really wants is the house, because it has so much of him in it. So, in exchange for her kindness, I gave her free use of the resorts."

He shook his head, remembering the way his step-mother's voice had trembled. He still wasn't convinced she wasn't a gold digger. All he'd really done was given her more money. He didn't care. By this time on Monday, he'd be on his way to getting his company back.

Christina pulled away, enough to meet his gaze, and frowned at him again. "Sebastian, that's millions you don't need to spend."

"Guess I'll just have to make sure profits go up next year." He winked, hoping she'd relax. When the worry didn't disappear from her gaze, he cupped her face in his hands, smoothing his thumbs across her cheeks. "I won't let him dictate my life anymore, Tina."

She studied him for a long moment. Just when he was sure she'd argue with him again, she arched a brow, a sassy, mischief-filled gleam in her eye. "I won't wait more than a month past the time limit. We've got two months to go still. I won't wait any longer."

He let out a quiet laugh and slid his hands over the curve of her backside, tugging her as close as he could physically get her.

"You're a stubborn woman, you know that?" He leaned down and nipped at her bottom lip. "Neither will I. Think you can plan a wedding in three months?"

She grinned, bright and beautiful. "Piece of cake. I've got

Hannah and Maddie. Mom will be thrilled. She'll insist on a huge wedding, you know. She'll probably take over the whole damn thing."

"Let her. I don't care how we get married. As long as at the end of the day you're mine. Though, I would like to take you to Vegas. Cade would probably tell me that Paris or Greece is more romantic, but I want you to have a better memory of the city. I originally considered kidnapping you again and flying you down there, but—"

Christina shook her head. "That's really sweet, Baz, but Hannah will be too close to her due date by then. I couldn't get married without her and Caden."

He nodded and lifted a hand, stroking her cheek.

"Exactly why I didn't. I *would* like to take our honeymoon there, though. You need to see that city the right way." She stared up at him, silent for a moment, her eyes glowing. Overwhelming relief tightened in his chest, and he crushed her to him, burying his face in the fall of hair at her throat. "God, when I woke up this morning, I thought I'd lost you."

"Me too." She turned her head, pressing her lips into his neck. "I love you, Baz."

Her words came as a trembling murmur against his skin. His heart roared and emotion overwhelmed him. His love for her. Gratitude that she was his, that he hadn't screwed up their relationship. He squeezed her so tight she squeaked, then let out a watery laugh. When he pulled back, he leaned his forehead against hers.

"I love you, too. So fucking much." His voice wobbled,

his overwhelming love for her caught in his throat. "You're mine, baby. You're mine, and I'm yours."

"For always, Baz. For always." She laid her head on his chest.

A quiet meow drifted from the floor, followed by the all too familiar brush of a small, lean, furry body against his right pant leg. Spike purred loud enough for the neighbors to hear as he wove his way through their legs.

Sebastian glanced down and laughed, then bent and scooped his best furry friend off the floor. "What do you say, pal? You okay if we keep her?"

Spike meowed again, and Christina let out a quiet laugh, glancing at Sebastian as she stroked the cat's head. Spike, of course, leaned into her, rubbing his head against any part of her he could reach. "I think it's official."

The love in her eyes took his breath away. She really was his. He had to be the luckiest bastard on the planet, and he planned to spend the rest of his life showing her how grateful he was to have her. And he'd start now.

Sebastian leaned in and covered her mouth with his. Christina moaned softly and leaned into him. His tongue searched for hers and with a quiet shudder, she reached back. He lost himself in her sweet lips, in her quiet sighs and the little trembles moving through her. When her hands found his waist and she pressed closer, Spike meowed in protest.

Sebastian broke the kiss, somewhat breathless, and nipped at her bottom lip. "Hold that thought." He set Spike on the floor, and he trotted off toward his favorite spot on the windowsill. Then Sebastian turned to scoop Christina off her feet and strode toward his bedroom. "It's still Sunday. We've still got a few hours before the weekend is officially over. I believe we have some making up to do."

She leaned in, tracing her tongue over the shell of his ear. "I can't think of a better way to spend the day."

Epilogue

You know, baby, at some point, we have to leave this hotel room."

Still panting, her body hot and sticky, Christina let out a breathless laugh. Lying lengthwise on top of Sebastian, she dropped her head into the curve of his shoulder. Their bodies had glued together from the heat and perspiration they'd worked up in each other. Beneath her, he lay with his arms tight around her, his chest rising and falling as rapidly as hers.

His hands stroked her back, calloused fingertips caressing her spine. "I didn't fly you to Vegas to stay indoors all week. We're supposed to be sightseeing."

They'd been married for three days. As she'd expected, the wedding had been huge. At hearing they were getting married, her mother had shrieked with excitement, then taken over the whole darn wedding. She'd demanded traditional. Among a sea of several hundred guests, most of whom

Christina knew only through her parents, she'd vowed to love, honor, and cherish this man until she died.

Her heart filled for what had to be the hundredth time since the pastor announced them as husband and wife. He was now officially hers, and she was his. They were happy. Stupid happy. His presence was everything her life was missing.

As promised, they'd taken his private jet to Vegas for their honeymoon. Sebastian had planned it out, including renting out the penthouse of the Bellagio hotel. On the flight out, they'd discussed all the grand plans he had for her, to show her the city. All the shows they'd see and sites they'd visit. He was like a kid in a toy store, filled with exuberance and an addicting joy at the prospect of making her better memories of the city.

Oh, room service came and went. They showered, chatted, ate, did normal human stuff. They'd gone so far as the spa for couple's massage, but they had yet to leave the room for more than an hour at a time. Once alone, they'd done what newlyweds do best—made love, then made love again. Clothing had hit the floor the minute the door closed behind the bellhop. They'd consummated their marriage in the room's foyer, against the wall.

She lifted her head from the curve of his shoulder and met his gaze. His hair was mussed, but his eyes glowed, with love and a touch of humor.

Unable to resist teasing him, she stroked his stubbled jaw, trailing her index finger over his bottom lip. "Why? I have everything I need right here."

His chest rumbled beneath her with his quiet laugh. "I'm sore, baby."

She giggled, heart full, and laid her head on his chest again. "I know. Me too. We'll go out tomorrow. I do want to see the Strip at night before we leave. Hannah and Maddie will never forgive me if I don't bring back pictures. And I promised my assistant, Paula, I'd bring her back a souvenir."

"And we have to do the casinos at least once."

"Mmm. Definitely. And Paris. I want to see the Eiffel Tower."

Silence settled over them, comfortable and luxurious. As their breathing evened and the sleepy lull of satiation and exhaustion rose over them, Sebastian let out a quiet laugh. "Seems you're now two bachelors short for next year's auction."

He was right. Her top two auction favorites had been taken off the market. She slid off his chest into the space beside him, snuggling against his side.

"Mmm. So it seems." She pressed a kiss to his chest. "Though I can't say I'm sorry for either one of them. Now that Hannah's had the baby, Caden's delirious he's so happy. Fatherhood suits him."

Two days before the wedding, Hannah went into labor. Little Emily Moira McKenzie arrived twenty-four hours later, quiet as a church mouse. Christina hadn't been certain how Caden would handle birth. He was cool as ice when dealing with work, but according to Hannah, he'd been a nervous wreck. Hannah had later confided that he'd had to take a seat. Twice.

She looked just like her father. A full head of dark hair and big wide eyes. He'd taken right to her. Every time she went over to see the baby, Caden had her tucked in one beefy arm. Yes, fatherhood definitely suited him.

"Cade's delirious because he's exhausted." Sebastian let out a quiet laugh, but as they lay there, he became a little too quiet and his body tensed. For Sebastian, quiet and tense meant he had more on his mind than he wanted to share.

Concerned, she lifted her head, sliding her hand up his chest to rest over his heart. "Tell me?"

He peered at her for a long moment, eyes working over her face, as if he really were worried about something. Finally, he drew a breath and released it. "I have to admit, I'm kind of glad you didn't end up pregnant. I don't want kids yet. Not never. Just…not now. I want to enjoy you for a while."

That weekend their relationship came to a head flitted through her thoughts. Sebastian had staked his claim on her at the cabin by the lake. Too caught up in each other, they'd forgotten the condom. As it turned out, her worry that she might be pregnant had been a false alarm.

She smiled, relieved that's all that worried him, and laid her head on his chest again. "Me neither. I don't think I'm ready yet. I'd rather enjoy this for a while, just the two of us."

His arms tightened around her, his body relaxing, and he kissed the top of her head. "I'm glad we agree. I was afraid to tell you. I've disappointed you enough. So, what do you plan to do about the auction?"

The familiar face popped into her mind, and she couldn't help smiling. "Oh, I know a certain bachelor who's been evading me. I don't intend to take no for an answer this year from Grayson Lockwood."

Sebastian laughed softly. "Please don't tell me you're play-ing matchmaker again."

She tried to be serious, she really did, but she couldn't contain her grin. He knew her too well. "What's the matter with wanting people to be happy?"

"You can't fix the whole world, Tina. I feel sorry for the bastard. He doesn't stand a chance against you. It's why I al-ways allowed you to volunteer me. You'd look up at me with those eyes, and I was a goner."

"I'm kind of glad I won't have to share you anymore. I wasn't looking forward to this year's auction."

"Mmm. Me neither." He hooked a finger beneath her chin, tilting her face to his, and playfully nipped at her bot-tom lip. "Now you're all mine."

Her heart swelled. "And you're mine."

He brushed a tender kiss across her mouth and resettled. Silence once again rose over them, comfortable and inti-mate. Christina closed her eyes, giving in to the luscious pull of sleepy satiation and contentment, and snuggled farther into his chest, letting his scent and the warmth of his body lull her.

"I love you, you know that?"

His voice drifted through the semidarkness of the room barely above a whisper, but so heartfelt and honest, tears pricked her eyes. If it were possible to love him any more…

She lifted her head, meeting his gaze, and brushed a soft kiss across his mouth. She was so damn grateful for him. "So much."

Please keep reading for a preview of *Bargaining for the Billionaire*, the next book in JM Stewart's Seattle Bachelors series.

Available September 2016!

Chapter One

Dread sank into Madison O'Riley's stomach as the musical jingle of her phone announced the arrival of a message. Any other day, that sound would bring a smile. It would've meant that she'd gotten a text from one of her two best friends. Usually Christina confirming details for a girls' night out or Hannah sending a picture of her three-month-old daughter, Emily.

Tonight, however, that sound meant the message she'd been waiting for had arrived. For a moment, she could only stare at the sender's name, blinking on the small black screen. Was she really ready for this?

"Is that him?" Seated on the couch across from her, Hannah leaned forward, bracing her elbows on her knees.

Maddie lifted her gaze, peering across the coffee table. Hannah grinned, ear to flippin' ear, her dark brows all the way up into her hairline. The rat. At least Christina tried to hide her excited smile. More refined, she sat with her long legs crossed and her hands folded in her lap. She looked calm and unperturbed, but the glimmer in her eyes gave her away. Both women were clearly waiting for the "deets."

Maddie sighed and shook her head. "How did I let you two rope me into this?"

Okay, so she knew the answer. Both had found their soul mates. They were all so damned happy it made her flat-out jealous. At this point, she was stalling. This blind date they'd "encouraged" her into should be a good thing. She hadn't dated in three years, and they were right. It was time. This hair-brained scheme provided a middle ground. After all, what harm could a little flirting do?

Hannah straightened, leaning back into the sofa cushions. "Because you're lonely, babe. You said it yourself. But you also said that you weren't ready for another relationship." She shrugged. "It worked for me. I got to know Cade online. Start there. It's just Gchat. If you decide you don't like him, you don't have to go through with the auction."

Christina flashed one of her smiles, the soft kind that always managed to melt the nerves raging in Maddie's stomach. There was something so calming about Christina.

"Hannah's right. There will be hundreds of women willing to take him off your hands. But he's nice. I promise. And he's not a *toad*, as you so aptly put it. I gather only the best for my auctions." Christina grinned, giving her a sassy little wink that had Maddie hard-pressed not to laugh.

Her two best friends couldn't have been more different. Where Hannah was quiet and shy and often uncertain of herself, Christina was all elegance but bold as brass. Maddie had known Hannah since her days of working in the marketing department of Bradbury Books, long before they'd taken a walk on the wild side and opened their little bookstore four years ago.

She'd met Christina through Hannah. Christina was Hannah's husband's twin sister. They'd officially become friends when Christina asked for help planning Hannah's bachelorette party. She'd made an instant lifelong friend that night.

Maddie hadn't known it at the time, but Hannah had been having an online fling. One that eventually led to her falling in love and getting married. Hannah had taken a chance and met Cade in person, and what began as a two-week fling had become more.

Exactly how Maddie found herself staring at a Gchat message from a stranger, nausea swirling in her stomach. She wouldn't exactly call herself celibate. After her breakup with Grayson three years ago, she'd sworn off men and dating. Which meant it wasn't raining men in her world, either. It didn't help that she'd trust another man when little pink elephants flew south for the winter.

Hannah reached out a socked foot and nudged her toe. "Oh, go on. Answer him. What harm can it do? He doesn't have your number, just your email address, and believe me, nobody in the world is going to know who Mad Hatter Three Thousand is."

Maddie's mouth went dry, a dull pounding starting in her temples. "Oh, God, I think I'm going to be sick."

Her hand trembled as she picked up her cell from the cof-fee table. She swiped her finger up the screen, then tapped the Gchat icon. The message that popped up was innocuous really, but her phone shook in her palm anyway.

BookNerd: Hey. Christina gave me your email address. Apparently, you're my date for the auction this year. ;)

Christina came from a wealthy family. As the founder and head of a local charity, which her family made a sizable do-nation to every year, her "baby" was a bachelor auction, in the name of raising money for breast cancer research. It was where Maddie had met her. Cade had been one of the bach-elors.

Twelve hunky guys were being auctioned off for a good cause. Any other time, she'd have been all over that. She had no desire to date, or God forbid, fall in love again, but she was a woman, after all. With needs and yearnings, and she missed things like sex. She had a sore need to get laid. She wanted the weight of a man's body pressing her into the mat-tress, yearned for a real cock pounding into her, hot and hard and not made of rubber. She wanted the huff of his warm breath on her neck, and by God, she ached for the luscious rush of an orgasm she didn't have to give to herself.

She'd grown damn tired of her own fingers, but sex with a real man meant complications, which she flat out didn't do. Flirting with a hot guy, though, could make her whole night. Knowing the men Christina chose for her auctions were all successful, with muscles on top of muscles, didn't hurt, ei-ther. Christina had excellent taste.

This year, Maddie had a date with someone she'd never

met and wouldn't until the night of the auction. Exactly two weeks from today.

She glanced down at her phone again. His username seemed harmless enough. It hinted that they had something in common—books. Her stomach still wobbled all the same, and she cursed her nerves. It wasn't like her to be so nervous. She was a people person, damn it. Besides, she couldn't stay single forever. If she truly wanted a night of hot, sweaty sex, she had to get back up on that horse. And it started with this damn message.

Her thumbs hovered over the on-screen keyboard. "What on earth do I say to him?"

Christina gave a soft, airy laugh. "You could start with hello."

"Hello." Maddie nodded. "Right. I can do that."

Oh, God help me, here goes nothing. Her fingers shook so hard she had to type the word twice.

MadHatter3000: Hi

She swallowed past the lump of fear stuck in her throat, punched SEND and waited. His reply popped up almost immediately, sending the butterflies in her stomach into an uproar.

BookNerd: How are you?

Maddie grinned. Okay, this was easy. This she could do. She punched in another quick reply.

MadHatter3000: Good, thx. U?

BookNerd: Oh, I'm fairly certain my night just got a whole lot better.

Maddie rolled her eyes. Oh, that was cheesy.

MadHatter3000: Ur a flirt, aren't u?

Once again, his reply was instantaneous.

BookNerd: Guilty as charged.

Across from her, Christina arched a brow in silent question.

Hannah sat forward again, bouncing on the couch like an excited child. "What'd he say?"

Maddie pursed her lips and lifted her gaze. "He's flirting with me."

Hannah's grin nearly split her face in half. "That's not a bad thing, Madds."

Maddie shrugged. The knots in her stomach weren't so convinced. "I suppose."

Christina smiled over the top of her wine glass, her eyes gleaming with playful impishness. "This is where you flirt back. If you want some company after the auction, you're going to have to leave a trail of breadcrumbs for the man."

Maddie laughed and shook her head. Christina was right, of course. If she wanted an orgasm from somebody other than her Battery-Operated Boyfriend, otherwise lovingly referred as to B.O.B., she'd have to come out of her shell a bit. After all, wasn't that what she'd told Hannah to do? When Hannah had been in the same place two years ago, trying to decide if a fling with Cade was what she wanted, Maddie had urged her to live in the moment or else she'd regret it. And Maddie had a lot of regrets. What would that weekend with Grayson have amounted to, had she not gotten cold feet?

She sighed. "Okay, okay. Let me think. I'm rusty at this."

She tapped her finger on the side of her phone, thinking.

The words popped into her thoughts seconds later, and Maddie typed and hit send before she lost the nerve to say them.

MadHatter3000: Confident aren't we? Don't think a date means ur automatically getting into my pants. ;)

She stuffed the nail of her index finger into her mouth and waited. Had she been too rude? Too presumptuous?

Seconds ticked by before his reply came back. Just long enough for the doubts to close around her throat. She had to be insane for agreeing to this.

BookNerd: Are you challenging me?

Her head filled with visions of what he must look like. Tall, dark, and handsome, like Cade and Sebastian. Full of muscles, for sure. And sitting somewhere doing exactly what she was—his phone in his hand, waiting on her replies. The thought had her heart hammering a giddy beat, and her palms sweating, but damn. This could be addictive. It was the most fun she'd had since...well, since Grayson.

Thoughts of her ex had the beginnings of panic clawing up her throat. Hands shaking in earnest now, Maddie leaned forward and set her phone down on the coffee table. "I can't do this. This isn't me."

Hannah set down her glass of soda and pushed off the couch, coming to perch on the arm of Maddie's recliner. She looped an arm around Maddie's shoulders, hugging her tightly. "Yes, you can. You're the first person in the store to pounce on any halfway decent-looking man who walks through the door. You're an incorrigible flirt. Why does this one make you so nervous? It's just a date."

Maddie shook her head, memories rising over her. "When

I flirt with the guys in the store it's just fun. I haven't had an actual date in three years."

Grayson Lockwood wasn't the first guy she'd fallen in love with, but that breakup had hit her the hardest. Discovering his lies had taken from her everything she swore they had and made her feel like a hopeless fool. She'd discovered on the front page of a local newspaper that he wasn't just another editor working his way up through the rungs of the publishing company they'd worked for at the time. He *owned* the company.

Her phone pinged again from the coffee table. She and Hannah both turned. Another reply flashed on the black screen.

BookNerd: Nervous?

"Do what you do best, Madds. He's just a guy, and you need this. You want this. You said so yourself." Hannah squeezed her tight, then released her and resumed her seat on the sofa. "Try being honest with him. Always worked for me and Cade."

Maddie sighed. She had to admit, Hannah had a point. Cade was good for Hannah. He'd opened her up and given her confidence. Hannah no longer hid the scars that cut across her face. The two of them were so damned happy Maddie couldn't even envy them. Hannah deserved to be happy. More to the point, if honesty worked for them, maybe it would work for her, too.

She picked up her phone, typing in a more honest reply.

MadHatter3000: I don't usually do this sort of thing.

BookNerd: Honestly? Me neither.

This reply soothed the knot in her chest. His confession, however, filled her with questions.

MadHatter3000: So y r u?

BookNerd: Because I told Christina the only way I'd participate was if she made sure I didn't end up with some 80 y/o woman or her lonely daughter.

Ah, now they were getting somewhere.

MadHatter3000: So, u don't want to do this, either.

Knowing her date didn't feel so certain either wasn't the most promising prospect she'd ever had, but the nausea swirling in her stomach eased by a large degree. At least she wasn't alone in her nervousness.

BookNerd: Not originally. I don't usually participate in these things. I have no desire to end up as someone's plaything. But I have to admit I'm enjoying this. I'm betting you're feisty. And clearly you don't trust easily. Truth is, neither do I.

Maddie smiled. Beginning to finally relax, she couldn't resist teasing him.

MadHatter3000: How do u know I'm not an ugly hag?

BookNerd: LOL I've known Christina since high school. I trust her judgment.

Hold the phone. Christina had distinctly left out that little detail.

Maddie peered across the coffee table at Christina. "You know him?"

Christina smiled. "Of course. You didn't think I'd set you up with someone I didn't? I've known him since high school. Gr—I mean, Dave is a nice guy."

Maddie narrowed her gaze on Christina. It had almost sounded like Christina was about to say another name. In fact, since this whole thing began, Christina and Hannah had *secret* written all over them. Their heads were always bent together, and they often exchanged grins that ceased the minute Maddie joined the conversation. She'd let them convince her it was nothing, but this time, she had to know.

She pursed her lips and pointed a finger. "All right, what is it you're not telling me about him?"

Christina held up her free hand in mock surrender. "Nothing, I promise. You just picked an excellent wine is all. I'm afraid I haven't indulged in a while, and this Moscato is delicious. It's going straight to my head." Christina glanced down, brushing invisible bits from her lap, and lowered her voice. "Thought I might be pregnant there for a while. False alarm."

Hannah nudged her sister-in-law with an elbow and shot her a grin. Christina flushed to the roots of her dark hair.

Momentarily distracted, Maddie couldn't resist a giggle. This was what had drawn them all together in the first place. They were all so much alike. Teasing came easily, and the laughter flowed freely. Now it had her mind shifting gears. Christina and Sebastian had been married almost a year now. Christina had married her brother's best friend. Having known each other most of their lives and been in love with each other for half that, the two were the poster children for typical newlyweds. They had a penchant for disappearing together. Christina always returned a little flushed. Sebastian

usually came back with a swagger and a grin, like he'd con-
quered the world.

"The point being…" Christina narrowed her gaze, eyeing
them one by one. "…I've known him for a long time. He was
always a bit of a loner. We're a lot alike in that respect. Growing up, he was a fellow nerd. Smart, worked hard to get good
grades. I've been trying to get him to participate in the auction since its inception, but he's always refused. This year I
managed to convince him, but only if I promised to fix the
game for him. He didn't want to end up with a date he'd regret or someone who'd make his life hell afterward."

Maddie arched a brow. "Isn't that cheating?"

"Yes, but it's for a good cause. The purpose is to raise
money and awareness." Hannah shrugged. "Besides, everybody always has fun, and there are eleven other bachelors."

Her phone pinged again, another message flashing on the
dark screen. Maddie squeezed her eyes shut, afraid to look.
"I still don't know if I can do this. Grayson took a lot out of
me."

"You have to get back on that horse sometime, Madds. If
you want to find Prince Charming, you have to kiss a few
toads." Hannah nudged her with a socked foot again. "Go
on. Pick it up and flirt with the man. Have a good time. See
where it takes you. It doesn't have to be any more compli-
cated than that. What's it going to hurt?"

Maddie opened her eyes and sighed. They were right.
She'd never be able to move on by playing celibate and dead.
She leaned forward, snatched her phone off the coffee table,
and peered at the message.

BookNerd: Did I scare you off already?

She arched a brow at Christina. "Is he really good looking or was that just lip service? Be honest."

Christina winked, mischievous and amused. "Oh, I think he'll make a *mighty* fine horse."

Maddie laughed softly. "You two are terrible, you know that?"

Only between the three of them would they ever say something so audacious, but it was what she loved about Hannah and Christina. They could relax around one another, and say things they might not otherwise. It made them excellent friends. She never held back with them. It was also what had made her give in to this date, despite everything inside her screaming what a bad idea it was. They'd always have her back, no matter what.

Hannah pursed her lips and waved a hand at her. "Oh, come off it. You're thinking it and you know it."

Maddie shook her head. "I am getting awfully tired of my B.O.B."

Christina and Hannah broke into a fit of giggles. Maddie drew up her inner vixen, beaten and worn out though she was, and typed in the first halfway playful thing she could think of.

MadHatter3000: I don't scare so easily. U just better have ur A-game on.

His reply arrived seconds later.

BookNerd: Ohh, sweetheart. Consider that challenge accepted.

Acknowledgments

Special thanks to my critique partner, Sharon, for going above and beyond. I could not have gotten through these edits without you.

And I have to give thanks to my editor, Jessie, as well, for challenging me to see outside my box and teaching me something along the way. Thanks for helping me make my baby shine.

About the Author

JM Stewart is a coffee and chocolate addict who lives in the Pacific Northwest with her husband, two sons and two very spoiled dogs. She's a hopeless romantic who believes everybody should have their happily ever after and has been devouring romance novels for as long as she can remember. Writing them has become her obsession.

Learn more at:

AuthorJMStewart.com

Facebook.com/AuthorJMStewart

Twitter: @JMStewartWriter